Other novels by this author:

A Pale Shade of Honor

Neige Noire

A Witness Too Silent

This is a work of fiction. Apart from references to the White Mountains and Morocco, the locations, characters, and storyline are drawn entirely from the author's imagination.

Mabbs-Zeno, Carl C.
     Birch Bark and Blackberry Thorn
     ISBN 978-1-7331262-8-1 paperback
     ISBN 978-1-7331262-9-8 e-book

Birch Bark and Blackberry Thorn

Carl Mabbs-Zeno

Khotso Publishing
Peterborough, N.H.
2019

Contents

DINER
Museum

Birch Bark and Blackberry Thorn

The ways of work and the wiles of women,
Scents of sweat and simanthea airborne,
Sweet sins of hell and saints of heaven,
Birch bark and blackberry thorn.

Chapter 1 - Morning Walk

Mud season! Charles' first thought of the day revealed his sleeping brain might have been aware of the rattle of rain but it was not the noise that awakened him so much as his habit of rising without hesitation at the same hour every day. On good days, like this one, he woke a minute or two before the alarm went off. He rolled toward the clock to watch with bleary eyes as the last few seconds passed until the radio came on. He slapped the button on the clock before the announcer uttered a full sentence. He sat up and listened consciously to the rain, visualizing it soaking into the remaining snow cover and melting out holes that exposed the dark soil in random patches. Although mud does not enjoy a favorable reputation for most people, Charles was pleased with the images it evoked for his morning walk: sodden, steamy, soft, slippery, and sensual.

Sensual? As he pressed his feet one by one into his slippers, he looked back at his bed to absorb its emptiness, lacking the tender warmth and presence of Natasha. It was painful that she was gone and he wondered that she had not been his first thought. Could he have gotten over losing her in less than a week? Was his new status already ingrained or was it, in fact, not a new status to be living alone, merely his normal status. She had been with him less than a year; longer than anyone else, but maybe not a new normal.

He padded stiffly to the window and leaned on the sill while he blinked to get his eyes working better. It was dimly lit outside by a streetlight on the opposite side of his house. He knew the melt of snow did not imply it was warm outside. He thought through what he would wear for his walk. It was a comforting exercise, knowing he had solutions to whatever the weather was doing. And if his solutions did not yield perfect comfort, he could endure, would enjoy enduring, whatever came up for the 30 minutes before returning for breakfast. He would take his dimmest flashlight to disturb as little as safely possible the elemental reality of the hour and the season. There would be the first stages of sunlight in his town before he returned, as viewed from space, but it might not penetrate the watery ceiling to any effect.

The rain would simplify his morning walk, removing the prospect of any wildlife sightings and the temptation to collect some natural oddity. His concentration would be directed at navigating his route without slipping on wet leaves or collecting too much rainwater down his collar. That might be enough to keep Natasha out of his consciousness.

Heavy wool socks over thin cotton, the light pair of long johns, loose canvass trousers from the bedroom closet, rain pants and the hooded raincoat from the hall closet, the tall boots from the floor in the hallway, baseball cap from the shelf by the door. His cap would keep the rain out of his eyes, but the bill might be wrecked by the soaking. He selected the cap he picked up in Glacier National Park four years ago; it was about worn out already. The hooded raincoat was not entirely waterproof so he could expect a wet shirt, but he wore three flannel shirts so it would be warm water by the time it reached his skin.

He stood in the doorway looking at the downpour backlit by the streetlight, the one he usually hated for lighting his nights, which he preferred dark as God intended the back side of the earth to be, but which was helping him this morning to appreciate the dramatic shift in season, from winter to mud; spring was still be a long way off. His breath formed a small cloud in front of him. A mild wind scraped the raw air against the skin of his face, a pleasant sensation to wake him more fully. He supposed that by the time it was no longer refreshing, he would be numb. The sound of the rain, heard in the doorway, mixed the dull drone heard through the roof with the higher pitched whine of rain on pavement and the dull hiss of the rain on the grass and snow of his lawn.

He stepped off the concrete pad in front of his door onto the gravel walkway to the street and squished onto the grass on his way to the back of the house. He could have used his backdoor to reach the path in the woods, but he wanted that view of the rain. He avoided looking directly at the streetlight so he would not burn out his night vision.

What the streetlight saw was the first human of the day to stir on the quiet, narrow, gravel road it had watched incessantly for forty years. The waking human was standing in the only doorway with no lamp at the door. All the others burned a light through night as if to welcome someone who might come knocking. It saw the same line of small houses on each side of the road, appearing much as they had been throughout its watch, but the steadiness of this view was false, a product of the lamp's poor ability to distinguish myriad tiny details that together would have revealed to a more discerning vision the fundamental deterioration. The houses were no longer painted regularly, their hinges sagged, much of their lawn space had given way to dirt, their families were older and less active. The lamp had noticed the reduced activity of its charges but had no broader experience to inform its analysis, to understand that the style of the homes and the cars that parked in their driveways had fallen greatly behind the times. These people were not poor, did not feel poor, but they had less than their predecessors and less than their neighbors closer to town.

Charles did not need the flashlight to find his way across the yard; a dark swath had formed where his tracks in the snow from earlier morning walks had compacted the snow. It was a slippery strip and he walked slowly to be safe. The wind pushed the rain into his face while he was crossing the open space of his yard. He turned his head to the leeward, but he could not turn entirely away from the wind and still see his way so his face was soon wet and a cold trickle ran off his chin and down the front of his throat. Quickly, as if to let no one notice his weakness, he tapped his chest to daub the thin stream with his shirts. It was an ill omen to be cold and wet so soon, before the adventure began. At the edge of the woods, he blinked to clear his eyes, still tired from sleep and getting numb from the wet wind, to see if his sight could be any better.

Not a photon emerged from the woods to guide him. Reluctantly, he switched on the flashlight and the world he could perceive instantly shifted from the hazy, open space of the yard to the small area immediately in front of him, an area without detail a moment before, but now recognizable as a revised version of the forest where he walked every morning, a steady visitor to his capricious friend.

The trail led down a steep slope to the stream. With so much rain, it would be too slippery to navigate safely, so Charles worked his way down the slope away from the trail, searching out the deepest patches of snow remaining. They held his mass but for a few inches on a few of his steps. He faced to the left throughout the descent, feeling his way as much as seeing where to go, and grabbing onto tree trunks or using the trees as footholds where it was convenient.

The stream was rushing with a roar. The heavy rain had brought its weight to the flood and the weight of the snow it had melted overnight. Charles stood beside it for a minute, playing the flashlight's beam up and down the flow. In the artificial and inadequate light, he could clearly sense the power of the surge, but could not recognize the stream as the one he saw every morning. The peculiar light was only part of the strangeness; the torrent was twice the size he had seen by moonlight the day before.

The path he normally took would be under water in places. Any route this morning would be a difficult ramble. The moments of watching the stream were thrilling, saturated with movement, noise, and the physical drill of rain on his head and shoulders, but it was also an ominous precursor to a dreary tramp without scenery, wildlife, discovery, or familiarity. Lacking a trail, Charles considered going back to the house directly, knowing there was no chance he would do so. He clamped his jaw tightly while forming an involuntary smile at the challenge to his will, a challenge he would easily surmount. It was not a significant trial to hike along the stream under these circumstances-- people had walked halfway across a continent to the South Pole. His test was one those people had not faced-- it was to go forward into the wet, cold darkness without prospect of new knowledge or personal glory while a warm house with stores of oatmeal and cocoa stood a few hundred yards away.

One foot and then the other and then back to placing the first foot one step farther on his way. There was nothing of significance inside the narrow cone emitted by the flashlight. He saw nothing outside the cone; he heard nothing but the rain and rush of water; he was confident nothing else was moving nearby at such an ugly hour. This simple exercise went on for much longer than his usual morning walk since he advanced so slowly, and it seemed even slower since he could see no sign of progress-- but the distance was finite and was eventually traversed. His first sign that his turning point was near was a change in the sound of water. The stream made many noises as it leapt over logs and stones or spread out over its banks, but these were distinct from the approaching deep, steady drone of the swollen Penobsconit River.

He turned off the flashlight and blinked a few times to help his eyes adjust to the dim light. The open area above the river let in a slight glow from the rising sun filtered through the clouds. He was relieved to see both time and space showed change. He would be near the end of the road where small boats could be launched. Guided only by the diffuse radiance, he hurried forward. Soon he saw the power lines that run along the road and cross the river at the boat launch. He planned to jog back to his house along the road, as much to warm up his wet legs as to get back as soon as possible, but he stopped suddenly before climbing up the slope to the roadway.

There were some trucks parked there, a very odd thing on any day at this hour, but especially in a downpour. He peered ahead, not sure why he was cautious. There were men moving around, talking incessantly. He was not close enough to understand what they were saying and did not really want to eavesdrop but he hung close trying to see or hear something to explain the odd rendezvous.

Suddenly he turned even colder. He recognized there was a figure sitting atop one of the trucks, with a rifle across his chest. The guard was watching the road, obviously not expecting someone coming from the river. Charles quickly realized there might be more than one guard, so he looked around more before moving back. He did not see any more rifles, nor did he see the road clearly, but he was very curious. He couched below the embankment, tucked in against a tree, his head at the level of the road, ten yards away, peering through a thicket of young, leafless trees. He could tell it was a green pick-up with a two-door cab and big fenders like trucks had in the Fifties. The other vehicle was a recent model, white, full-sized van. A car farther away was dark in color, but he see no more than that it was a sedan. He could not read the license plate, but could get its color and see the number consisted of two digits, a dash, and three more digits. He understood a few words. The only ones that seemed significant were "New York," "Montreal" pronounced in the American way, and a man's name: "Robbie." They were moving crates into the van and the truck. They might have already sorted the cargo on some basis or were making a trade from one vehicle to the other, he speculated. Maybe the crates had come in from the river, although it seemed insane to ride the flood.

He noticed a man walking along the edge of the road, coming toward him, apparently patrolling their perimeter, carrying a rifle. Charles slouched down further. He doubted he would be visible. Moving away would be more conspicuous than just sitting in place and watching, but the light was getting stronger as the sun rose higher behind the clouds. The guard moved past. Charles waited another minute and then backtracked. The rain drowned any noise he might have made moving through the wet woodland. He worked his way through the woods before cutting away from the stream to the road a half mile from the river,

nearly where it met the state route. He wanted to be
back in his house, cooking two eggs over easy while
sipping hot cocoa. His legs felt strong, inspired by
adrenalin. They begged to run, not from fear but for
the simple use of their power. He could only hold
them back temporarily. He jogged forward onto the
black road, plashing through invisible black puddles
without hesitation, except that whenever a car's
headlights showed he stepped away into the bushes.
He wanted no one to recall seeing him this morning.
In 15 minutes more, he was back on his own street.
From this day forward, he would take a different route
for his morning walks.

His 30-minute morning walk along the stream had taken an hour. He had seen far less than usual, except for when he saw far more than he wanted to see. He did not know what he had seen and he knew before his knees had been warmed by the shower that he would not be reporting what his imagination had perceived though the mist and discomfort and mental exhaustion very early on a muddy Monday in March.

Chapter 2 - Consulting on a Baby

The shower promised to end his hypothermia. He set the water to be less warm than he liked it, just to be sure it was not hot enough to damage his numb flesh. He stood under the shower head and waited for sensation to return to his extremities. His knees, in particular, felt alien. His fingers and a few of his toes burned as they regained their circulation. His morning routine was running late but he did not hurry. The odd events he had witnessed merited review. He spread the washcloth across his chest, as if he were dressed by that action, and lingered in the warm rush of water. He tried to understand what he had seen, but he could not control the topic that came to his consciousness. He replayed his most recent exchange with Natasha...

"Charles, we need to talk." Natasha had said that phrase twice before and both times it had been about the same thing and there was no good in it.

"Sure, Baby. What about?"

"You say you love me."

"I say it and I mean it. You are the best thing that ever happened to me, Dear, the finest women I ever met or imagined."

She looked at him sternly, straight into his eyes. Her accusation did not go unstated—it was stated in her face. YOU DON'T LOVE ME! His answer did not go unstated— it was given clearly by his silence. After giving this answer, he asked gently, "What do you want me to do?"

What he did not want to do was to become part of anyone else, her, for example. He wanted to remain himself at times: to walk in the woods alone at his own pace for as long as it took to empty his mind of what was preying upon it and to saturate his mind with the timeless, undemanding, naïve, anonymous innocence of fen and forest; to kick his muddy shoes onto the carpet and deal with the consequences later, if at all; to stay up until 2 am working on a project when the project was working well and then sleep in late the next day to recover, not that he wanted to sleep excess hours, only that the particular hours he slept be chosen by the exigencies of the moment; to make bad decisions about matters affecting his health, when they were consciously made, like eating well-marbled meat charred on the grill or drinking beer in the morning when it is hot despite the hour or getting a flu shot or not when the mood struck him in a given autumn.

Twice before, this conversation had ended without catastrophe. It had ended with her apologizing for demanding he be someone other than himself. On the first occasion he had been shocked by the whole direction and content of her attack, for it was an attack on his claims of love and, equally, on his interpretation of what love is. On the second occasion he realized nothing had been resolved on the first occasion.

Having no good answer to her interpretation, he was relieved when she shifted into her apology, but he knew the matter was not closed. He had then thought about what he would answer when it came up again. He did dearly want her to remain with him. Was that not love? He wanted her to be at home to tell him about her day and broaden his experience thereby. And to be interested in his day and tell him how clever he was to have done whatever he did since they last met. At the moment of the conversation, as in every other moment when he focused on her, he completely wanted to bury his face against her skin, anywhere would do, and to have her want his desire and to know how to inflame it further and to join him in extinguishing, however temporarily, his animal passion. Maybe that part was not love exactly, but his persistent interest in exploring her body and none other was widely recognized as associated with love.

When the conversation began for the third time, he was disappointed. He had hoped it would not have returned so soon. He even had a slight hope that it would not have returned until he had an answer for her. But here it was again and the best he could do was avoid denying what she knew to be the truth, given her parameters on the meaning of love. He could communicate his despair at her needing a form of commitment he never had and could not offer. That had been enough on the first two occasions to end the confrontation. This time, she was prepared for his passivity. She rested her arms on the table and sat squarely facing him, looking into his face but speaking to herself in a low voice: "My mama done tol' me, ' a man'll sweet talk and give ya the big eye, but when the sweet talkin's done, a man's a two-face, a worrisome thing who'll leave ya to sing the blues in the night.'"

Charles smiled at her tuneless recitation.

"You're not even a man; you're just a boy. You may never be a man." This was probably a thought she had planned on expressing. It apparently summarized her view well. It was not something he could argue. How can he argue against a statement the speaker knew was objectively false? Her real point was that he was not what she wanted. And if that was true, she was not what he wanted. So he let her leave while she was asserting he was "passive-aggressive" as if that term were so damaging to his ego that he would amend his ways.

Fortunately, he ran out of hot water, forcing him to end his masochistic reverie. At least it had washed away the questions about his morning adventure. Today's wet walk in the dark now seemed unreal or even inconsequential. He was energized by ridding himself of that imagery and by running out their last conversation again, leaving no agenda of thoughts to be thought.

By 9:00 am the rain was over. The soil was fully saturated and mostly thawed, just as expected in the weeks before the equinox. With an egg and ketchup sandwich in his belly, and a job all set for the next couple days, Charles was back to feeling normal.

His old van scraped its tires against the curb, causing poor Charles to fear they had just lost a thousand miles of wear. He couldn't afford to buy a new tire-- new tires; they probably needed to be bought in pairs so they would wear evenly. Not if he were going to get a new Skilsaw before his next job. He had a list of things to get over the next year and a budget for getting them after paying for his rent and his meals, and saving a fixed amount for investment. The Skilsaw would be bought from the profits on the current job, the painting job.

The irritation passed quickly, as an act of will, of self-control, seeing himself getting mad over a simple and small driving misjudgment. Rubbing tires on the curb was not worth the effort of pumping extra blood under his collar. His budget was not that tight; he just wanted so much to stay on his plan. He wanted that Skilsaw because he knew it would pay for itself within a few months. Or, he thought, maybe he just wanted the pleasure of a more professional tool replacing the cheap, awkward model of hand power-saw he had used for the past four years. The tools, like the work, were largely ends in themselves. He took no pleasure in buying consumer goods, he enjoyed the way tools extended his capabilities, as if he were himself more capable, as if he had learned something or trained himself further. It was, to him, an acceptable illusion:

greater self-worth with the expansion of his tool kit. He was, in fact, concurrently learning his trade and training himself to do more, and no one, including himself, could say how much of his improvement in work came from buying better tools, improving his skills or even just working harder.

Painting did not require expensive tools although such tools existed. He knew there were spray painting machines run off air compressors. They could be used for exterior painting; as far as he knew, they might even be used on interior jobs like the one at Apartment 347B, 15441 Oxen Cart Way. But better tools for painting were not in his plan. In fact, he did not intend to be a painter. It was something he did as part of a larger job or when he had a gap in his workload. House painting was mentally undemanding and therefore boring or relaxing, depending on his mood. On this day, he was planning to be relaxed. The whole job would last two or three days, he guessed, and he would shift from prepping to taping to painting enough and he moved to various rooms that he did not lose interest or get too achy from repetitive motions.

He sat his hand-truck beside the van in its horizontal position and loaded his equipment on it, everything but the paint. That should already be inside. He had agreed with Mrs. Bowers on the type and quantity of paint, and she had bought it. The arrangement removed any concern about the price and color. Charles liked his customers, but he did not like spending time with them and participating in the color selection was entirely a waste of his time although his customers sometimes wanted his opinion. Catering to their insecurities about color choice was akin in his mind to the medical quack's relationship with a hypochondriac.

"Mrs. Bowers!" Charles called out as soon as she stepped outside. He liked his customers to know he liked them. "Today's the day!" He did not really have anything to say to her. He had confirmed everything with her by telephone.

"Let me help you," she answered back. Charles did not want anyone helping him and he refused to patronize Mrs. Bowers by pretending to accept her help although he was not sure if he could avoid leaving doubt that her help was particularly unwanted, she being slow, weak, and obese. Painting was a job any fit person should be able to do. It took more very common sense than skill and few tools. It was especially unchallenging in a shabby apartment where the standard of quality was universally low. She had too little money to be hiring him. She had a husband who looked relatively fit and several teenaged children. She had left the door open in her waddling rush to help him unload his van and he could hear the voices of some teenagers inside.

"Yes Ma'am. I can probably use a hand here. Of course I won't be paying you a wage for the time you put in."

She smiled and Charles felt good for going against his principles about patronizing her. He took a couple old sheets off the pile of drop cloths. "It would be good if you could carry these in. Half the time they fall off my cart when I'm wheeling it in. They slide around, being so soft and shapeless." The description would have been more apt for her and he hoped she would not think he had tried to be clever and insulted her. He had spoken the words with honest intent; the second meaning came to him as if he were a bystander, hearing someone else talking.

The front door opened directly into a dark living room, crowded with thick furniture. Mr. Bower rose from the couch briefly to shake Charles' hand and murmur some words of appreciation. His attention was fully refocused on the television before Charles had crossed the room. Charles wandered through the rooms he would paint: dining room, two bedrooms and a small bathroom. The living room and kitchen were no better than the ones he was doing, but for unspoken reasons, they would be untouched.

Four girls were giggling in one of the bedrooms, three teenagers and one slightly younger. The young one was probably a sister and two of the teens would be friends visiting. He thought one of the teens looked related to the young one. The girls followed Charles back into the dining room and stared at him as if he were there to entertain them. "I think I'll move all the furniture into the blue bedroom and put all my stuff in this room. Then I can start painting in the bathroom. That'll be the hardest room to do. You won't be able to use it for a few hours so you might want to get in there now." They looked at the room but did not move toward it, as if they were afraid of missing some part of his performance.

"You know, I told your Mom, I guess she's somebody's Mom, I told her the whole place is going to smell like paint once I get started." Still they looked at him silently, as if waiting for instructions. However, they were not motionless, looking constantly back and forth among themselves, as if communicating in some other plane. Charles smiled at their embarrassment and tried again to break the ice. "Which of you is a Bower?"

They all raised their hands and then, a second later laughed loudly, bending over and spinning around while still each of them held one hand high, as if waiting permission to let it down. One of them said "I'm a cousin," and another added, "Me too."

"Very cute," Charles added and turned back to his work.

Mrs. Bower came in and challenged the girls to make themselves useful, loudly proclaiming this would be a good time to show they were as mature as they claimed to be by showing some responsibility. Charles looked at their carefully selected clothes, meticulously painted fingernails and stick-skinny arms, and knew they were not about to volunteer to help with his painting. And Mrs. Bower knew it even better than Charles. Oddly, the girls seemed uncertain. They stepped forward and asked what they could do. The tallest one said she really wanted to learn how to paint. And yet before Charles could finish saying how messy it would be, they had all fled back into the bedroom. He stood at the door and mentioned again that the house would soon smell of paint. It would not be toxic; he was using latex, but it would be strong. He could see them inside their room, already as remote from his influence as the images on the television entertaining Mr. Bowers in the other room.

Charles cleared out the bathroom. Judging from the toothbrush rack, Charles figured five people were sharing a single shelf to store their personal and intimate objects and chemistry, so unaccustomed to privacy that none of them bothered to move anything aside in preparation for the stranger who would be in their home all day. Charles was quick in piling it all on the bed in the other room. He counted two beds in each room and supposed the boy he had not met yet slept in the room with his parents. It was not an unusual arrangement when viewed by global standards, but Charles, who did not think he had grown up among the privileged, did not know anyone who lived quite so crowded.

The bathroom needed the most attention. The old paint had not been designed for steam and had peeled away in large patches. Also, the ceiling needed some significant spackle repairs, and the tile grout was either broken away or yellow with mildew. He fixed the ceiling first, ignoring the underlying reason it needed to be fixed. The thick sections of spackle would not be ready to sand down until the afternoon. It knew should be painted before the walls but the priority was to get the room back in use as soon as possible so he resolved to be very neat when the ceiling was ready to be painted. He did his minor repairs to the walls and grout and then told everyone the bathroom was available while the plaster dried.

The dining room needed less preparation and he soon had it ready. He stirred the paint can and poured a couple inches into the roller pan. He went around the edges with a brush, working his way around quickly with a short step ladder. Then he screwed the roller onto a long handle and pulled his cap back so the bill would not block his upward vision. No ladder would be needed to do the rest of the ceiling. He was aware of a light spray that flew off the roller onto his face and the drop cloths. It reminded him of how foolish it would be to paint the ceiling after the walls in the bathroom. They could use it but should not move their stuff back into it this day.

The tall girl came out of the bedroom to watch him. Charles warned her that she would get paint on her just by standing near or by walking on the drop-cloths, but she was content to stand on the other side of the room. She asked him to explain what he was doing. It seemed pretty obvious to Charles and he did not want to be distracted by conversation. Nonetheless, he placed a high priority on common courtesy, so he turned his attention to her while resting on one knee. The girl was attractive. She had an adolescent's body, but carried herself as a woman. Her skin was smooth as a baby's, dark as British tea, and glowed deeply. She wore hair extensions that had been expertly worked into her braid. She was much too young for Charles to think of enjoying her company and much too old to regard as a child. His tactic was to bore her.

"The way to get a decent paint job is to prepare it well. Patch the holes, sand the edges, tape the borders carefully. Little mistakes and shortcuts on these things will be conspicuous forever. And then go around the sides of the ceilings with a brush 'cause the roller can't reach all the way to the corner." He looked at her with peripheral vision. She was paying some attention to him. "Once you get it prepared for the roller, it goes pretty fast."

"Is that thing heavy?" she asked, referring to his roller.

"Nah, you can't say it's heavy, but when you start doing the lower parts and don't need the extension handle, it feels a lot easier."

"OK. Thanks," she concluded, as if her question filled in the last gap in what she needed to know and she bounced back into the bedroom and closed the door. Charles was not sure if she were now satisfied that she knew how to paint or if she were able convince the others of her new skill. Maybe his strategy to bore her had worked.

With the girls' chatter subdued by the closed door, Charles could hear the television more clearly. Mr. Bower was watching a shopping channel. It was pitching outdoor furniture. Charles figured he had gone to sleep on the couch. Next came an ad for a footstool that opened for storage of many suggested items one might wish to have nearby. Then came an especially husky voiced salesman offering a certain radar detector for those who wished to speed without getting caught. He made the police sound no more significant than mosquitoes at a barbeque. Mr. Bowers stirred from the couch and called the station to order one of the radar detectors for $68.00. Charles felt a little less bad about charging for his work if his customer could make such a spurious purchase and then he wondered if he should not feel even worse about taking payment from someone who was such a sucker.

By mid-afternoon, Charles was transferring furniture from the bedroom into the dining room. The boxes of clothes that had nearly filled all the floor space in the bedroom were stacked both under and on top of the table. The beds and mattresses were in one stack and the bureau took up the rest of the room. One had to walk sideways to pass through the room, but no one complained or even acted as if there were anything unusual in that arrangement while passing by to get to the bathroom.

Charles could tell the job would take longer than the two days he had planned, and he saw some good in this. He was charging by the job, based on a theoretical hourly rate and an estimated number of hours. Now he could see he was giving this crowded family a better deal than intended and he would feel no guilt regardless of how much money the old man wasted.

As he taped around the edge of the ceiling, he listened to the chatter of the girls in the other room.

"How about Leslie," said one of them who was greeted with a sudden chorus of high pitched groans indicating a consensus that Leslie was not the one.

"Well, I always liked Laurie," said another.

"No, no, no. Lindy's better."

"Yeah, yeah. I like Lindy too." And then the voice said "Lindy" very slowly.

"Maybe I like that. Do you ever hear of a 'Lindy'?" No one had.

"Good. I don't want a famous name."

"Charlotte's no good, right? But how about Charlateen? Don't that sound feminine?"

"Ooh, that's sweet!"

"Yeah, Charlateen!"

"No, no. Say it Charlateen," and the girl pronounced the "CH" as in "church."

"That sounds like "Charlie. There was perfume called 'Charlie' and it was a woman's name."

"How can you spell that?"

"That man out there is 'Mr. Charles'. Ask him how to spell it."

When his name was mentioned, the girls must have realized they could be overheard and dropped their voices for a hurried negotiation. Charles heard the door to their room open and a faint patter of feet on his drop-cloths while he waited for their question."

"'Scuse us, Mr. Charles," someone began weakly.

He held his wet brush up so the paint would not drip off and turned around.

"Yes?" he answered firmly. "Charles is my first name."

"I know that," the tall girl answered. She was the group spokesperson. "Uh, Mr. Charles, do you, like, know how to spell Charles? I mean I know you can spell it, but do you, like know some other ways to spell it? Can you say some way that interesting?

"Do you think I spell it in a boring way? I'm a cool guy, you know. Maybe I changed it along the way from the boring version my mother gave me."

"I dunno..."

"If you thought that, you would be right. I do spell it in a boring way. My version is the French way. The most unique thing about my use of 'Charles' is that I call myself 'Charles', never 'Chuck, Charlie, Chaz, or Chip'," There are so many options because this name was so well respected at a certain time in Europe. Do you know what famous person was called Charles?

None of the girls answered or even moved.

"Anyone?"

He waited a moment, certain they would not answer, but the tall girl softly muttered, "No."

"Have you ever heard of Charlemagne? That is French for Charles the Great. He founded the Holy Roman Empire."

"Charlemagne sounds nice. Is that a girl's name?"

"No, Charlemagne was a guy. And it is a name only the original bears. But many generations of boys were called Charles after him. And many boys in German areas were named 'Karl' after Karl der Grosse, which is the same name in German."

"Oooh, that one sounds terrible, but at least it sounds like a guy."

"I think 'Karl', spelled with a 'K', is the original version, from the German for 'warrior' but Americans usually know the man as Charlemagne. If you are looking for a cooler way to spell it, there are versions in every European language, I am sure."

"No, that's not what we want. We want a name for a girl, but a special name, like she is the only one with the name spelled her way."

"There are feminine versions of the name. I think you would find them too familiar."

"How do you spell 'Charleteen'?"

"I would spell it the easiest way, so the girl would not have to struggle all her life to communicate: C-H-A-R-L-E-T-E-E-N, I guess. Maybe you could have an 'A' after the 'L'. But this would not be the most unique way. Of course, I have never heard that name before, so maybe it is unique enough already. In fact, I think that is a pretty good name for a girl."

"Tamara's pregnant," announced the young girl, apparently indicating the tall girl's status.

"Congratulations," said Charles, carefully avoiding any tone that might be interpreted as ironic.

Tamara, the tall girl beamed proudly. "It's a girl. She's due in July."

Charles carefully did not look at her belly. With her slim figure and tight clothes, her pregnancy should have been conspicuous, but he had not thought of it before.

"So what would you call a girl?"

"I would think of people in the family to honor. Did you consider relatives? It might be cool to find a feminine version of your Dad's name, for example."

"I don't hardly know my Daddy. That man in there is not my Daddy. He's just Mama's husband, like, her second husband."

"Sure. That's OK. You asked what I would do."

"What name do you think Tamara should use?" asked one of the cousins.

Charles had a sudden inspiration, but he did not want to delay his work further. He pushed his brush into the corner and stroked downward, spreading paint on the edges of two walls, where the roller would not quite reach. "Tamara... Three syllables ending in 'a'. I'm thinking of a name with a similar sound. 'Seneca'. It was,,, is the name of an Indian tribe."

"An Indian name?"

"Did you see the movie 'The Last of the Mohicans'? The Seneca were the westernmost of the Iroquois. They fought alongside the British in the movie and in history." Of course the girls were unlikely to have seen the movie but far less likely to have read the book.

"Seneca?"

"Yes, it's unique for a girl, don't you think? And it sounds like 'Tamara,' too." Charles imagined a baby girl bearing the name he has suggested throughout life. Wouldn't Natasha be surprised when he told her someday.

"Why use an Indian name. That's kinda like a football team or something."

"How terrible to have such a first association with Indian names. The rivers and towns around here are all Indian names. Besides, 'Seneca' is also a Greek name. Seneca was a famous ancient philosopher."

The girls were through with Charles. Too didactic, he knew. He kept painting while they whispered among themselves. Teenage girls were not his forte.

Finally Tamara spoke up. "Thank you Mr. Charles. We'll think about it."

Charles knew he had lost his chance to boast of this day to Natasha. Hey, he even noticed 'Natasha' has three syllables, each ending in an 'A'.

Chapter 3 – A Minor Theft

On a good day, one when Charles got out of the house early on his way to a job, he stopped at Smiley's for coffee. It was not the best coffee ever brewed but they did not serve donuts and he could justify going out his way to avoid being in a room full of temptations that would waste his daily calorie quota. As time passed, he had to acknowledge to himself this perfectly adequate justification was not true. He went there to see the cashier. He always had a snappy sentence for her and she always had a brilliant smile for him, although he never pushed the boundary of the client-cashier relationship. He knew he could not be disloyal to Natasha since she was now gone but he felt cheesy to explore the cashier's availability. He had never made a date with someone he did not already know. She smiled at everyone and, Charles imagined, everyone felt richer for it. She was an extraordinary person in an ordinary place. She had the huge eyes of Ethiopian art and the cocoa skin of people from the Arab-African mix common along the Red Sea. Her smooth, innocent face made her seem very young, and Charles was surprised when he first saw her standing that her body bore the fullness of maturity. Yet Charles was certain she was not yet a mother and he doubted she was married. Without any flirtation, she communicated her availability. Charles wished he knew she was married so he would not feel pressure on himself to see if she might be available to him. But if her innocent visage were real, he would have to imagine himself fitting into her view of how life proceeds and it would surely not be consistent with his. It seemed so reasonable to ask her out, and go someplace interesting and learn what she liked to do and talk about. Somehow, early in the relationship, he would have to address his curiosity about why she was in this small New England town. Could there be any explanation other than that she had married a New England guy she met in college? Or a Peace Corps guy in her home country?

On his way to the coffee shop, Charles thought of whether he would get something more than coffee. He knew that asking himself this question nearly always resulted in answering himself in the affirmative and moving on to the question of what he might have for breakfast. He tried to answer that question with as few calories as possible. His taste in breakfast fare ran quickly to a full day's quota. Usually he talked himself down to an English muffin, toasted bagel, or a croissant. These seemed roughly equivalent and gave him a choice, but they signaled a compromise to his weakness. This day, he decided to forego the bready options in favor of getting a larger coffee than usual. Drinking an extra-large coffee one day would not, he calculated, excessively deepen his dependence on caffeine.

That was the core of his plan as he parked the van in the small lot beside the shop. Next he needed to think of something to say to the cashier. He always choose innocent topics like the weather or the day of the week, never something that assumed a particular cultural background, like the world series or a new movie, and never something that could be interpreted as prying into her personal affairs. He did not even know her name. He had once overheard a customer caller her "Elizabeth," but he assumed this was only a name she used to be more easily understood by the local folks. He sometimes, not too often, greeted her saying "indemin allesh," which is Amharic for "hello" when greeting a woman. It was the only Amharic he knew. She would answer to it as if it were his first language but she never tested him to respond any further in Amharic.

He casually looked in her direction when he got inside, prepared to wave if she turned his way, but she was not at her post. He recognized the woman at the register as one of the waitresses. He went to the coffee urns to fill a large paper cup and used his peripheral vision to scan the room to see if the dark woman people called "Elizabeth" was wiping off or a table or otherwise occupied. The room was not large and there were only two other customers so it was easy to see she was not there. He put in one extra sugar and squeezed on a plastic top. Disappointed at missing his morning visit with the beauty, he strode quickly toward the register while reaching. Only there was no wallet.

He had only tapped himself on his back pocket; no one watching him could be sure he was looking for his wallet and he smoothly kept walking over to the counter where pastries were displayed. He looked through them and wondered what he was going to do with the coffee. If Elizabeth had been there, he would have asked to borrow the price of the coffee. She might have agreed. He wished·he had put some money for emergencies in the van. The emergency money he carried was in the back of his wallet; not a good place for solving the present emergency. He sipped the coffee while he eyed the pastries. He sipped some more coffee while he went to shelves where candy and snacks were displayed. He drank about a quarter of the large cup and then walked past the trash can and dropped it inside. With empty hands he walked out.

In the small parking lot beside Smiley's Charles heard someone call his name. He knew no one from the diner would care if he stole a coffee, but it was so far outside his normal range of sins that he felt a melodramatic surge of guilt and irrational fear. In an instant, however, he recognized the voice of his good friend Hemo.

"Yo," Charles answered.

"You got time to pick out a breakfast for me?"

Charles realized that Hemo could have paid for his coffee if he had delayed just one minute more.

"Bad timing, man. I'm on the run this morning. Besides, my favorite cashier's not in today, so what the hell."

"All right. Later, man."

Chapter 4 - Hemo

The next few weeks continued in the usual way for Hemo but led to some resolutions. They typically consisted of frustrating days, days of mind-numbing drudgery and relentless disrespect. Hemo did, as always, what his boss asked him to do and he did it consistently well but his boss asked him only to do the strenuous, dirty, repetitive tasks as if Hemo were a mule entirely untrained and inexperienced in their business. Hemo suspected his thick neck and broad girth made him appear too much like a pack animal. He had expected to advance to better jobs with time, but he would have been satisfied in the near term by some diversity in his work to allow him to prove himself. Each day he came to work with slightly less hope to find an opportunity for change.

He sometimes weighed his options for an hour after collapsing exhausted in his bed at night. Find another job? He would have no recommendation likely to help him get a better job, and he knew no one yearning to give him a break, and he knew of no job opening his skills might fill. He had skills, he knew. Besides being strong and reliable, he was capable of attentiveness, honesty, extended effort, and, maybe, occasional brilliance. Or so he thought and who could know otherwise if he never had a chance to display his rarer attributes? In those late night reviews, he developed a cogent approach to improvement of his situation. He would focus his attention, which had no particular application on a normal day, to finding some way to improve the *process* of work; some step in the process that could be simplified, some insight that could be drawn on the small pad of paper he would start carrying in his shirt pocket, some suggestion that would avoid embarrassing anyone while benefitting his boss, maybe by reducing his crew time or material. And since he was not an eager novice with more ideas than common sense, he would hold his fire until he had a winner, a surefire proposition certain to distinguish him in the eyes of his peers and his supervisor.

Hemo bought a pad of paper and a mechanical pencil which he carried to work every day for a week. He wrote down six ideas in that first week, more than one a day, but none of them struck him as worthy enough to become the foundation of his step forward. It was good practice for him to make some notes and to rehearse, while lying abed nursing the aches and scrapes accumulated during the day, making a presentation of them to his boss. In these rehearsals, he was modest, but confident, insistent without getting overly aggressive, casual and well prepared.

In the second week of his approach to advancement, he was about to make another note when he realized the new observation was a variant of a note he had already entered. It had cropped up twice, making it a pattern. It was time to step forward. He was not shy. He wondered why he had not initiated more interaction with his boss. Just being better known individually would help his chances for improvement. He was a personable guy; people liked him; except maybe not good-looking women so much.

The boss was a hundred yards away along the road from where Hemo was laying pipe. Hemo looked down at his shirt and considered tucking it in but thought that might be pretentious, so he walked toward the boss in unadorned honesty. His sweaty, dirty, loose clothes were testament to his contributions to the project so far this day.

"Oscar!" he called as he approached the boss. His voice came out weakly, which surprised and embarrassed Hemo. No one heard him, which was probably for the good. When he was closer, he called out again in a richer voice driven from his diaphragm: "Hey, Oscar!"

"What's your problem now?" Oscar answered, an inauspicious opening to the conversation Hemo had wanted for two weeks, a tone Hemo did not deserve since he had never complained of anything. Hemo stayed cool, knowing the boss liked to be bossy.

"I've been laying out the pipe on the right down there. You know, draggin' it along the ditch 'til it can be put in the collar of the last piece?" His voice went up, making this a question. The question was "Are you following me?" Or, maybe, "Are you paying attention?"

"Yeah. I know what you're doin'."

"I was doin' the same thing over on Ryder Street last week. Working with Jon, kinda. He's a ways ahead of me doin' the same thing."

"Yeah, I know what he doin' too. I know what all of you are doin'. So what?"

"Well, draggin' the pipe is the slow way to move it. It gets hung up against the sections already in place. Sometimes it catches a rock underneath and you end up draggin' that one too, diggin' into the dirt like a plow. The pipe is always in the lowest part of the ditch so the back end of the piece you're draggin' pushes against the pieces already there. It can knock them out of place."

"You want a different job? Something easier?"

"I'm not lookin' for something easier." Hemo almost diverted the conversation to Oscar's question, almost answered that he sure did want a different job, a harder one if harder meant more brainwork. But he had rehearsed this conversation and knew he needed to get his point across in a way that made it clear he was doing something to benefit Oscar. "I bet Jon and I could move the pipeline a lot faster if we worked together. If we each took an end, we could lift the whole thing easier than draggin' it, and drop it in place exactly. One of us, the one on the back end, could insert the pipe into the line while the other one went ahead to the next piece and wrapped a strap in the end to help when we lift it. Smooth like a machine, you

know. Taking turns front and back. Moving along.
You think we should try it that way?"

"You think you invented a better way to lay
pipe? I've been laying pipe around here for twenty
years. Where were you twenty years ago? Suckin'
your mama's tit?"

"I was too old for that twenty years ago and
never did meet my mama. She died when I was born
and I grew up in an orphanage." Hemo lied about his
mother and he was starting to get hot. "But that's not
your problem. What do you think about changing the
way we put down the pipe? Just try it awhile and see
how it goes?"

"If you don't have a mama, where's you get that
weird name, 'Homo'?"

"I don't know why they called me 'Hemo'. I
do know 'Homo' is the name of man: Homo sapiens.
Oh yeah, and people stopped calling me 'Homo' back
in seventh grade."

"OK, sorry. Just kiddin'. Stupid, isn't it? You
wanna work with Jon, go ahead. As long as he don't
mind. See if you can make up the time you spent
coming down here and talkin' about it."

The exchange was not as supportive as Hemo
had visualized during his slumbers but he thought it
might have served its purpose. He had been noticed in
a way as positive as was realistic in the rough business
of highway construction. It was later, at the end of the
day, that he began to more seriously doubt anything

had been gained. He had focused on getting Jon to cooperate (Jon was as bored and muscle sore as Hemo so he was entirely willing to try a different way of working), and had not noticed Oscar leaving early. Hemo was certain they had laid out more pipe by the new method, but there was no way to prove it. They could do it again the next day, but Hemo had wanted feedback. Oscar's rude words grated. Riding in the back of the company pick-up from the worksite to the parking lot where he left his car in the morning, Hemo replayed the conversation in his mind and thought he saw that Oscar had retreated when Hemo pushed back on the name-calling. He thought this reflected a fundamental understanding that Hemo could punch his lights out if provoked. But that was not a tool for advancement. Oscar would not be intimidated into doing Hemo any favors. And thus, it was not really an unusual day, merely slightly interesting for having a new source of frustration.

He took a long hot shower in his apartment. It would have been better if he could have sat down while the water poured over him, relaxing his tired muscles, but the shower stall was too tight for a chair or to sit on the floor. He dried himself off and looked at himself in the mirror, flexing his biceps, and turning to find the best angle. He did not see Adonis in the glass. He was thick and proud of having earned most of his bulk, but he was not lean enough to display the cords of muscularity that lay under his hide. The ratio of his waist to his shoulders was not attractive. It was unfair that he suffered the pain and toil of physical work without gaining the beauty such effort imparted to others. And yet, he could see in his body that he was stronger than most people and anyone could tell this. It was something to respect.

As soon as he came out of the bathroom, he flopped naked onto the bed. He closed his eyes without bothering to lift his feet onto the mattress. He shivered, grabbed the blanket, and rolled over to cover himself while getting his body entirely on the bed. He was still cold. The blanket twisted over him and did not cover him well. He was not sleepy, only tired. He sat up. Through the open door of his closet he could see his midnight blue shirt, his favorite, offering to accompany him on an outing to find a comforting woman.

After a very informal meal, taken while standing in his kitchen area, Hemo went out to his car. He sat with his hands on the wheel for a few minutes, thinking of where to go. The seat was very comfortable, better than the chairs in his apartment, and it was invigorating to have the machine around him capable of taking him where ever he commanded. The moment soon passed as he could not name a place he really wanted to go.

The Saturn Grill would take him. He could blend in as if he wanted to be there. They had a TV that would give him a reason to face in a particular direction and would give him something to think about.

And it was just possible, though he had never taken advantage of it before, that a good and available woman would turn up. Available women had been there before. Even a few good women had been there, at least, they had seemed good from where he had sat.

Hemo parked the car near the Saturn. He considered it a bad sign that there was a space so near. It would probably be too quiet inside. A small neon sign reminded all that the Saturn Grill was open. Hemo was aware that the sign was a cheap option; it would have been better to have a blinking sign to proclaim the name of the place.

Inside it smelled slightly more of beer than grease. There were two televisions showing a professional basketball game. Hemo did not follow the sport although he knew the names of the major teams and generally how well the local one was doing. He could watch it and even comment from time to time to whomever was nearby.

He stood at the door and looked around casually to select his seat. He tried to project an image of a man looking to see if anyone was there that he already knew, darting his attention quickly from place to place, staring nowhere for more than a moment. No one looked back, but he went to the effort of tilting his head sideways to show he was disappointed that no old friends were there before moving confidently to a seat at the bar. He had been here before and knew this seat would give him a view of the TV without losing track of anyone else at the bar. There were two women a few stools away. They did not seem to be with anyone. He examined them in his peripheral vision while pointing his eyes at the game. One of them glanced his way and then turned her back to him. The two movements seemed connected. He had shown neither interest nor disinterest in her. It was unnecessary for her to reject him out of hand. Her new posture blocked any view of the second woman. He deserved to have a glance and resolved to find an excuse to walk around the room somehow, just so he could decide whether to look further into either of them. They did not need to be beautiful to be worth his effort, but they would need to meet certain standards in several categories. He could not name the categories or describe the standards, but he knew they existed.

Two fellows rose from their seat at a table and sat at the bar next to the women. Obviously they were interested, but the women did not react and the two fellows acted as if they just wanted a better view of the game. Hemo considered asking them if they even knew which teams were on the screen. He would have liked to embarrass them since they had essentially stepped in line in front of him. He could not be angry with them since he had not given any sign of interest in the women, except that anyone with experience in a place like the Saturn would have understood every movement he had made since opening the door.

Hemo was proud of his seat selection. He could look over the interlopers innocently while they could not assess him without turning away from the TV. Someone missed a dunk and the basketball bounced a long arc into the stands. Hemo groaned in sympathy, but more than that, he groaned as a conversation opener. A decent man would have turned his head at this point or uttered some other sound. Regardless of the team one favors, a spectator always understands the irony of a dramatically blown dunk. Hemo's friendly gesture was ignored. The two fellows whispered. Hemo was certain they were working up the courage to address the women. If they waited much longer, their window would close. They would be noticeably awkward. They had the advantage of having sat across from the women before moving their seat so they knew better than Hemo what was at stake.

One of Hemo's rivals offered the women their bowl of peanuts. It was a silly gesture. Anyone could get peanuts from the bartender at any time. It was an opening meant to appear gentlemanly but was in fact false. They should have said something about the game. That would have been an obvious invitation to talk. It is what Hemo would have done if he had seen them from a better angle and decided to meet them. The women did not take the peanuts, but the nearer one rotated her body so it was not rudely rejecting them, now that they had met. The two men appeared not to notice this opening and they faced the bar and whispered between themselves. One of them said something to the women; Hemo could not tell what it was. They answered with a wave and, a moment later, collected their change on the bar, put back an amount for the tip, and left. Since they were leaving anyway, Hemo dropped his disinterested persona and looked at their direction. The light was not good, but he decided at least one of them would have been well worth an effort. He would have made the effort, he knew what to do, except that the two inept men had gotten in the way.

Without any subtlety, the two men watched the women depart. One said something quietly to the other and then both looked at Hemo. Hemo turned his head away from the television and they slowly redirected their gaze back to the door where the women had exited. The closer one looked back to Hemo and Hemo asked with menace, "Watter you lookin' at?" He said it loudly enough for anyone in the bar to hear. He figured it was a good opening, one he had used to good effect before. Since he has asked this before of people he did not like, it took no effort to devise an approach to vent his anger at the whole day. He had communicated clearly and engaged someone in his troubles. In fact, it would have taken more of an effort to not ask the question in this mood, given there was a viable candidate nearby to give or take a beating.

Hemo looked tough and was acting tough. Clearly it would be a bad idea to antagonize him further... unless one wanted to prove oneself. In that case, responding aggressively back to Hemo was a perfectly logical response... especially if one has a buddy willing to ensure a degree of safety and assurance to revenge in the event of initial defeat.

Hemo was showering at his apartment thirty minutes later, without a woman waiting to touch his cleaned flesh. He did not mind the bruises he had acquired. Nothing on him, not skin, muscle, tendon or bone was torn, cut or broken; that made it a successful outing. He would have two days to recover before the workday began again. They would not be successful days either.

He sensed no immediate prospects, but he was not entirely lacking in resources. It was 2 am, Saturday morning. Good enough time to call a friend. He tapped in the number. The call rang three times and went to voice mail. "Pick up the phone, you lazy bastard. Then call me back." He did not put down the phone but sat with it in his hand, expecting it to ring momentarily, and it did.

"Hey, Hemo," said Charles without enthusiasm.

"Oh hey, Charles. Sorry to wake you up."

"Think nothing of it. I was only sleeping anyway."

"Look, I am fuckin' bored. Not at this minute. Bored for the weekend. Let's do something next weekend."

"Bored, huh? I am really sorry to hear that, my friend. Lovelorn, are ye? Alright, you're no different than me. Next weekend then. First thing on Saturday?"

"Yeah, real early."

"Bring Amin. And wear some boots."

"Thanks, man. Get some sleep. Whadda ya doin' up this hour anyway?"

Chapter 5 - Charles' Cabin

Over the crackle of frying bacon, Charles heard the front door open and then several soft footfalls. His friend Amin had a light step. "In the kitchen, man, working on your breakfast. Most important meal of the day, you know," he called out.

Amin was pulling his sweatshirt over his head, having dropped his coat on the floor in the hall. His voice was muffled by the struggle to strip down to his T-shirt. "Don't smell like my breakfast. What you got for a sometime Muslim? Shit, it's too hot out there already." It was 50 degrees, but Amin had been dressed for the early morning temperatures of the past and this was nearly ten degrees over yesterday at six am.

Amin had all the physical attributes of a lady killer: tall, smooth skinned, with thick dark hair and bedroom eyes. It had always been too easy to find a girl willing to give herself to him that he had never learned to value feminine company. So he was unattached and did not regret it. When a young man eschews sexual companionship, a tremendous proportion of his time and energy are freed up. His slender build and graceful movement gave him an athletic appearance but he had never had gone far in any sport. He had matured faster than his classmates and winning had come too easily when he was young so his interest in competition, athletic and otherwise, waned for lack of challenge. Schoolwork was not as easy for him but he had accepted its importance and applied himself assiduously, earning grades the brighter students envied and felt were unfair. But his teachers and college entrance examiners knew he was a good boy, not a scholar, and he went to a third-tier school with his self-respect intact but no substantial career in view.

"Hot? Not hot, I am sure. My thermometer says it is 48 and I heard it's going up to 60 today. The season had to advance at some point and today is the point. And in honor of the rare day, I have made oatmeal. Not instant oatmeal, real oatmeal, like my grandmother might have eaten before walking two miles through the snow to school when she was a teacher. Oatmeal and orange juice. What could be more traditional in New Hampshire?"

"How is orange juice traditional in New England? It must have first come here in the 50's when they had rails to Florida."

"Funny you say it that way. I would have said rails *from* Florida; you know, 'cause they carry the juice."

"The rails carry the OJ north, but the rails themselves spread from the North."

"They did? Where you get that? Didn't they have trains in the South to carry the cotton to the coast?"

"Who the hell knows? I don't know what's traditional. I've only been on earth, and self-aware, for a couple decades and didn't study much. And I don't know much about oatmeal. I thought it was a joke, like something tasteless but cheap. Like the next girlfriend you gonna come up with."

"It's cheap, but I would spare no expense for you, my friend. Careful, though, it will it stick your lips together."

"Speaking of lips, you know Hemo is outside sucking on a cig, right?"

"What's his problem? Does he think this is hallowed ground? HEMO! HEMO!" Charles walked to the front door. "Hemo. Don't show so much respect to my place. Mi casa es su ashtray.

"Fuck you, Charles. I am not steppin' on the wrong side of Natasha," said a voice through the open front door."

Amin called out from the kitchen. "Hemo, You been away too long."

Charles explained the recent history briefly. "Natasha's wrong side? This's where I live. She's gone, man. Nothing's left here."

"That's bad, Charles. Bad stuff. That was a fine woman," said Hemo as he came through the door, no cigarette in hand.

Charles nodded to himself although his head movement might have been visible to his two friends if they were looking at him. "I think that is why she left.

She was right to have a higher standard that anything around here."

"She wasn't like that. She..."

"I'd really rather not review Natasha with you sweet fellers. Really. You want some bacon? You can have half of Amin's share."

"Is this that healthy fake bacon Natasha cooked?"

"Nah. This is the real deal. The kind Amin can't eat so there's more for you and me."

"What's he sayin', Amin? Since when have you been holy?"

"Not holy, Hemo. I've been hearing that the pig is nasty all my life so it doesn't seem like a good thing to put inside me."

"You thinkin' too much, man. It don't seem like a good thing to put inside me either, but if I just eat it, it tastes real good," answered Hemo.

"Hemo's diet advice! Hemo's advice for life!"

"Yeah, I'm thinkin' of puttin' it on some bumper stickers."

Charles and Amin often teased Hemo about being big. It was a safe joke because he was not sensitive about his size. In fact, he was very comfortable being the largest person in almost any gathering who could still play a decent game of hoops. His belly drooped a bit, but it did not hang over his belt. He looked strong and was strong, although not strong enough to go far in the sports he had tried.

...Strong enough to impress his peers in the junior ranks and to build a self-image as the intimidating member of his tribe.   His eventual sporting disappointment left him in doubt of his self-worth and he was left to play the residual role of a jock that he never really had been. He was the sort to establish his rank when he walked into a bar and it had cost him more than a few bruises to keep up the persona he felt compelled to wear. He felt comfortable when he was with people he knew since they knew he was to be recognized as the toughest in the room, even if there was doubt that it mattered. But he felt most alive when he came across someone to challenge his physical superiority. He did not often pick fights, but he did sometimes insist on clarifying rank with anyone who refused to acknowledge it. With his two best friends, Amin and Charles, there was no issue of rank. They knew the struggles Hemo forced upon himself for lack of finding a better identity. His friends understood who Hemo was, and they liked him, but they did not know how to move him onto an easier path.

Charles wanted to get on the trail early. He did not have any distance goal for the trail; in fact, he wanted to feel like they could stop at any time or take a side trail or climb a tree if it might offer a better view. And yet he felt the urge to get started and he knew he would press the pace once they were on the trail so he could see past one more turn in the trail. Besides, he had an unstated goal worrying the back of his mind, a place he wanted to revisit. He prodded them to eat their oatmeal quickly by wolfing his own down in minimal time and dropping his bowl in the sink without any polite waiting as a proper host would do.

"I'm driving, since I haven't told you where we're going today. And I'm leaving now. Have you filled up your water bottles already? Or do you cowboys tote canteens?"

"This here motherfucker totes a few warm beers. They work out good on a cold day."

"Amin said it's hot out there."

"Well, Amin's a freak, obviously."

The three friends went out to Charles' old van just before the sun broke over the horizon. A pink light reflected off clouds rippled like a projection of details from an arthropod's underbelly onto the deep blue hemisphere above. All three of the young men looked at the sky on the short walk to the van. They all bathed in and were silenced by the odd color of the predawn light. The ephemeral atmosphere heightened their senses. The cool air was dry enough to be brittle. Every sound was magnified. They each trod carefully to minimize the crunch of gravel. The van doors emitted twin clicks as they were opened and heavier twin clacks as they were shut. Charles pumped the gas pedal once before turning the key because he did not want his van to hesitate in front of his friends. They did not speak as Charles drove to the end of his street. He almost laughed at the silliness of the sound of his turn signal. He checked in the rearview mirror and then looked to his friends sitting on the bench beside him. They were both staring forward, embarrassed at their own sentimentality. In another moment Hemo would find something stupid to say, just to display his disconcern for the dawn. Charles broke the hypnotic drone of the engine with the loud crank of the emergency brake.

"It won't last long. Might as well see it while it's here."

Charles leaned out the open door of the van while Amin got out and Hemo twisted around in his seat to peer through the back of the van. Of course, Hemo could not see anything through the distant rear window; it was too much for him to display interest in natural beauty, even with his best friends. He was aware of his weakness, but he could not overcome it. Amin held onto the door on his side. He and Charles saw the pink extend across the meridian, chased by a gold hue on the stationary ripples hanging inexplicably overhead. They watched for 20 seconds as the clouds faded to shades of gray and a blinding orb lifted its weight past the perimeter of the rotating earth.

"Let's go before the credits start rolling," Charles called over the top of the van to Amin and Amin nodded his acquisition although no one could see him.

"Whaja see?" Charles asked Hemo as he started the engine.

"Not a goddam thing. Don't tell me about it either. Next time I'll get my butt up."

"It's up to you, Bud," Charles concluded and they were on their way.

The van would rattle pleasantly on a smooth surface but clanked disturbingly on the rough and narrow roads it took from Charles' poor neighborhood, along the state highway for a few miles and then onto a tarred road announced by a sign with a four-digit number in lieu of a name. The rugged road showed fresh injuries it had sustained during the frost season as well as the hasty, uneven repairs of the past several winters. It was not a road important enough to justify repairs until passenger cars felt their lives were threatened by using it and the passenger cars in this part of the country were a tough lot, not easily intimidated and not prone to complaining.

"So where the fuck are you takin' us?" asked Hemo goodnaturedly.

"I was wondering if either of you cared to know. I did not figure you for the planner among us." Charles hesitated before answering the question in case Hemo wanted to retract it.

"Oh no," Hemo jumped into the opportunity. "Don't sell me short. I'm a big planner. I'm plannin' to follow your lead all the livelong day and then we'll get back to the van when its dark and getting' cold and we'll all be strung out and you guys'll pussy out so I'll drag my own ass to that crummy bar over on Avenue B and look for a woman to talk to and maybe take home with me but it won't happen. ...Again."

"I apologize, Hemo. You are a meticulous planner."

"And then I'll sleep to noon tomorrow 'cause I stayed up 'til that crummy bar closed 'cause there will be some woman, probably a fake blondie, who'll be startin' to look better and better as I git drunker and drunker, and I'll start to think, against all odds, that she lookin' back at my sloppy ass like I was somethin' she needs for the night, but I'll never actually say an actual word to her and that will be a good thing because I'll know deep inside I'm lookin' at her with the wrong organ in my body and when I get her in the light of morning I'll be embarrassed for myself and fearing she gets ahold of my phone number while she's getting dressed and I'm fakin' like I'm still sleepin' so I don't have to say nothing to her."

"There's a fine line 'twixt planning and predicting, Hemo."

Amin added his comment without turning his head from watching the trees go by. "I see how your plan ends with whatever woman you find falls in love with you."

"You think it's vain to expect the dog you find at 2 am wants to hang onto me? Maybe I am vain 'cause that's what I 'member often 'nough t'expect it."

"Pepper Falls," said Charles, his plan forced its way out of his subconscious and past his lips.

"What?" asked Hemo and then he clarified himself, "What the fuck you talkin' about?"

"Pepper Falls," Charles enunciated slowly and distinctly.

"It falls if you drop it," said Amin. "He's saying, Hemo, in his minimalist way, that's where we're going."

"Pepper Falls? Are we supposed to know it? Have we ever been there before?" asked Hemo.

"Pepper Falls" was a name Charles had made up when he found the falls a few years ago. He had looked on a topo map and found a dotted blue line marking the unnamed, ephemeral stream and two short diagonal slashes marking the unnamed falls. His name came from the need to hurry back on day he found it. (You know how "pepper" means doing something fast in sports, say baseball or jump rope?) He had been excited to find a waterfall of significant height not civilized by the presence of any trail and committed himself to returning, possibly with a friend or two. The map code designating the stream as ephemeral explained the lack of trail access but it did not diminish the value of the falls in its season. He returned in the summer of that first year and struggled most of the afternoon to find the stream. Although he had tried to be aware of the location when he left it that first time, returning in the opposite direction with the trees leafed out was utterly confusing. The long dell with the stream was duplicated in general features throughout the forest. Eventually he convinced himself he had found the right dry bed and followed it uphill for 30 minutes, challenging his conviction he was in the right place, but finally succeeding in finding the worn stones where the falls had been. He enjoyed the certainty of ending his search but was disappointed that the place looked so plain. And yet he was intrigued by the contest to find it again at its peak, in early spring.

Charles pulled the van aside the road onto a gravel parking lot with room for two or three vehicles, depending on the vehicles and their drivers. He kept to the edge to make room for two others, even though his van was larger than the usual car. "There's an old road here. We'll take that for a couple miles."

"Where's it go?" asked Amin as he tightened the laces on his boots.

"More than most roads, this one doesn't go anywhere at all. And it does not take long to do it. I've been to the end. It had no side roads. It just a leftover from yesterday."

"When's it from?" asked Hemo.

"Don't know. I have no idea when it was first used; can't say it was ever built. It's just a track that goes the easiest way it can sometimes and the straightest it can sometimes. But I've some idea when it was last used, that is, last used for practical purposes. There're some relics along the way."

"That sounds great!" Amin enthused. "What're we going to see?"

"It's not a museum tour. There'll be nothing to write to your mamma about, but you won't need to be a scientist to figure out some of the past. It hasn't been covered up by the present as much as in most places."

Charles strapped on his day pack with lunch for them all. He was counting on getting water later from the waterfall to wet their palettes. It was a small risk to prove, to himself, his confidence that it would be flowing full this day. There had been no rain for a week but the spring had been wet before that and the weather had stayed cool. He regarded the dry week as the start of the new season, spring after the mud.

"Before we start out, let me collect all electronics. This is a day with Mama Nature."

"That's *your* dream, man," said Amin. "I can handle the weight."

"It's about freedom, Amin. You need to assert it in full from time to time, just to remember how it feels. Sure, we haven't the big, dramatic threats but there is so little cost to leaving the phone behind and so much to gain. It focuses one on the present time and place. They are all that exist when you are miles from all human influence."

"My worries travel with me, but I'll agree to turn off the phone. I prefer the phone to be off anyway."

"It is not the same thing. Getting no calls is one thing and giving up the chance to send any is something else."

"I am not a follower of Teddy Roosevelt's and Ernest Hemingway's vision of nature: a challenge to be confronted; a proof of one's worth, if not of one's manhood."

"What if we need help?" asked Hemo.

"Exactly!" Charles happily shouted. "That is the critical thing! Getting a call is minor. I would not take that from you if you wanted it. Not if it was not too common. What is important is to depend on ourselves. Independence has its burden, a welcome burden. In this tame place and mild season, we could not find any major danger if we tried, but it is good practice to be off the grid for the day."

"You lack imagination if you think nothing could go wrong, if you can't think of some way some help would be nice. One of us could break a leg, get bit by a snake, drink some bad water, get appendicitis, attacked by a bear, poisoned by a spider, uh, captured by aliens, uh, I don't know. I don't have that much imagination... Oh, here take the phone. I don't know what the hell you're goin' on about but it doesn't matter to me. Like you say, there's nothing to worry about anyway. So leaving it behind doesn't do anything."

"Well I can't give you my phone," added Hemo. "It's back in Amin's truck. But I didn't leave it there 'cause of your retro philosophy. I just left it there.   Who needs it?   Who needs fuckin' philosophy?"

"You're beautiful Hemo," answered Charles. "You have most succinctly stated your worldview. I am humbled by the clarity of your vision and the economy of your words. 'Who needs fuckin' philosophy' indeed."

Amin hung a canteen and a bag from his shoulder. He was more concerned about unloading his hiking pole from the van. It was notched with half-inch increments for about two feet on one end. He inspected that end. He had a facetious theory that he could hike the New England forests until he wore the pole down to a walking cane. He imagined mounting a handle on the upper end when there was one half inch to go at which time he would be eighty years old. He was not worried about getting there too fast; he was worried that he would not hike enough to wear it down in time.

Hemo was not carrying anything. He liked the freedom of hiking empty-handed and, more than that, the freedom of hitting the trail without any preparation. He did not see it as risky; he was confident Charles and Amin would be excessively prepared.

Charles stretched his trunk, twisting to the left while grabbing his right elbow to feel the pull on his lats a bit more. Then he twisted to the right for symmetry. He bent forward to touch his toes and then grasped his ankles and pulled his face to his knees. He jumped up a couple times and finally screamed, "GOT-DAM! I feel good!"

"Like I knew that I would now!" Hemo called out and he drifted slowly backwards shuffling his feet in a dance that only looked bizarre to Amin.

"What are you doin'?" Amin asked.

"So good! So good!" answered Charles and then Hemo chimed in on the "Ba-ba-ba-ba-BAAA.

Charles shook his head at his own antics and explained to Amin, "That's from the Godfather of Soul. If you don't know him, it can't be explained to you."

"That's OK. I don't need to know everything," and Amin started walking down the dirt track.

Hemo started after him but Charles went back to the van to get the jacket Amin had shed and tucked it into his pack. Charles thought that Hemo was not dressed warmly enough to be comfortable if they sat for lunch or if the weather turned worse over the next ten hours.

The road began in a rare flat area of forest, displaying dual tire ruts. It might have been in current use as a fire road, giving access to more remote areas for firefighting. Even though a few bushes in the middle proved few vehicles had not been this way in recent years, it would have been passable by any of the popular SUVs that dominated modern interstate highways. It might have served as a logging road, but it was more passable than needed for that task. The past was written in the landscape and an earlier agricultural origin was likely.

Hemo broke the silence with a thought that had been brewing since they started out. "I'm not buying that freedom excuse."

It was obvious to the others that Hemo did not expect them to know what he was talking about so they waited for him to explain. Meanwhile he waited for them to ask for clarification. It seemed the courteous thing to do. After a few seconds, Hemo saw they were not going to ask and was disappointed. It was not just the courtesy of it; he did not care about that. It was that they did not seem to care what he was talking about. Or was maintaining the appearance of caring the same thing as courtesy? He answered the unspoken request for clarification. "You know, that we should leave our cell phones 'cause it makes us more free."

"Have you seen through to my actual motives for getting you out here without any way to contact the outside world?" asked Charles.

"Yeah, I get it. You like living in the past. I don't mean your own past. ...The long ago times, like when the stone walls were built. You like doing everything with your hands. And you can do things by hand; more than anyone else. But you're not so hot with modern technology. You prefer things made of nature."

"Do I? There is something in what you say. Maybe I am not fully aware of my motives. But normally I do have a cellphone."

"And normally, I know it, you don't like that cellphone."

"I hope I do not have a very strong emotional relationship with it one way or the other. So Hemo, did you notice the drinking glasses we used at breakfast this morning?"

"I don't remember them. I remember I drank some orange juice. Thanks for that."

"They were really cheap thick glasses, like the ones in a diner. I got them because they reminded me of a diner."

"You are making Hemo's point," suggested Amin. "Your taste lies in the styles of the past."

"I want to address Hemo's assertion that my taste leads me to dislike modern technology. In addition to the style issue, I also like the glasses because they are cheap. And in addition to that, I like them because they are glass, which does not leak when filled with liquid and do not harbor germs and are easy to clean. If I had to make with my skillful hands, a vessel as good for holding orange juice as that glass, I would not know where to begin. ...Especially if I had to make it from nature rather than repurpose some man-made item. If I somehow learned to make and shape glass, it would still take hours and hours to make the first one. And I paid, oh, say, a buck fifty for one of those glasses. I like to think I earn fifteen or twenty bucks an hour when I am working so that glass, if I already had the skills to make it, would cost me maybe a hundred times more in time than it did using modern technology, including construction, transportation, and marketing."

"I didn't mean juice glasses when I said you did not like technology. Juice glasses aren't technology. Not like cellphones."

"Maybe. I acknowledge that I like to be around technology I understand. I can't fix a broken glass, but I can understand what makes it break and how it works. A cell phone is a constant mystery. There is an element of taste in ditching my phone. But I like being out here without any phone, or camera, or radio so we can live in the moment. Not in the year. But for our clothes and our thoughts, look around you, this could be any point in time, past or present, over thousands of years."

The three young men tripped along happily, too full of energy to fully enjoy the setting, they could only feel the strength of their bodies carrying them slower than their capabilities.

"Hey Amin! Pull my finger!" Hemo knew he was being childish, but he felt safe in this with his friends.

"What are you talkin' about? What's wrong with your finger?" Amin asked.

"If you don't pull it, I'll have to pull it myself!" answered Hemo with an upbeat voice.

"Well stop a minute. What happened to your hand?" asked Amin with mild concern.

"Holy shit, Charles. He really doesn't know!"

"You'll have to show him. Amin, in some ways you were fortunate to be untrained and inexperienced in the pre-teen culture of American boys, but some aspects of it really are needed in life. This particular stunt has its own musical connection, but no soul. Hemo, show him the finger connected to the stress factor."

They stopped walking and gathered ceremoniously together. Amin leaned back unconsciously revealing his distrust of the situation. "You're not going to hit me, are you?"

"Never, my slender friend. Why would I, why would anyone ever hit you," and Hemo held out a hand with his ring finger extended. "Slowly, firmly, gently, if you please."

Amin looked to Charles and Charles nodded affirmatively. Amin pulled the finger and. Of course, Hemo farted boldly. Amin looked at Charles accusingly, and Charles shrugged.

"Hold on there, cowboy." Hemo responded indignantly. "I appreciate you helpin' me and all, but you can't be makin' faces with Charles about it. Fartin' is natural. It's as natural as that sunrise you liked so much..."

Hemo was just getting warmed up, but Amin interrupted, "That sunrise smelled a lot better."

"Bullshit! We're on the trail, man. You couldn't smell a thing from five feet away. And if you did you would only be smelling nature. Don't pretend you never farted. Everyone farts, even Muslims."

"It is a minor, pervasive evil. I suggest, however, very few cultures find it endearing to participate in the farts of others."

"And I suggest, that is precisely why the finger thing would be amusing in very many cultures. It is a smart trick to get someone to participate voluntarily in someone else's fart."

"Smart?" Amin said and then caught himself. His thought was to satirize Hemo's facetious claim, to ask him if scatological humor was any culture's notion of smart or if it was only his personal view, if that was the level of smart he had achieved at this point in life, if... But it would have struck Hemo's transparent insecurities, not an appropriate riposte by a considerate man. "Does it work with any finger? Can anyone do it?"

"Oh no," Hemo was pleased with the questions. "It takes talent. You have to have control of the gas, holding it without causing suspicion and then blasting it loudly at the right precise moment."

"I'll practice," offered Amin. The topic did repulse him, not inherently, but he thought he would momentarily degrade his dignity by embracing it. He felt generous for doing so. "You might want me to march third in our line for a while. Since you clearly emptied the tank, it should be safe enough for you to be in front."

Charles knew the road was too tame for a woodland hike, but he had chosen the route to get them quickly a few miles away from civilization before starting the proper part of the expedition. His hunger for a wilder place proved Hemo's point about technology so he did not mention it. The three kept their hasty pace, with the cool morning air and their fresh legs. They admired, each in his own way, the high canopy of empty branches over their route and the stout arboreal pillars that held it up. The huge volume enclosed, imperfectly, by the forest made the three hikers feel small. Yellow light from the newly risen sun angled steeply through the lacey vault into their space, furthering the ethereal atmosphere. They marched silently, but for the rustle of the dry leaves marking each step of each man. The sound was common enough to them but it was not usual to hear it continue for 20 minutes, nor to share the white noise with others for so long. None of them was able to break the spell cast by the simplicity of sound, sight, movement, and purpose.

Charles uttered the first intentional sound in thirty minutes as the road dropped steeply. "Spring," and he pointed a moment later, when his companions looked to him, with a nod of his head toward the side of the lowest point of the road. He walked over to the place he had indicated. There was a small ditch below the road and he climbed down to it a few paces. There was nothing to see until he pushed the leaves aside with his boot, revealing a few large rocks. He knelt on one of them and bent down to scoop away more of the leaves. More rocks could be seen. A little water shone from the below the rocks. "See? The rocks purposefully line a small pool. There used to be a minor dam on the end of it and this place could be used to fill a bucket." The three faces leaned in to share the sight of a small trickle tracking over one stone at the lowest point of the coarse construction. A faint sound of moving water rose to their ears from below the leaves. Charles put his hand to the trickle to collect some water but it was too shallow for him to get any into his palm. He lay beside the water and kissed the tiny flow, feeling the cold tasteless sweetness and drew it into his throat. He took a few swallows and sat back up, more refreshed than the quantity of water could justify.

"Who made it?" asked Hemo.

"Don't know," answered Charles. "Who made the road? Did you notice how it goes straight up and

down the slope, not following the contours at all?
'Makes it prone to erosion and harder to use."

Hemo and Amin regarded the road as if for the first time, as if they had not noticed it was nearby. It now looked more like history than transportation. Hemo involuntarily grunted out a syllable that reflected his mild interest in the new point of view. Amin asked Charles how he noticed the spring.

"It was pretty obvious when I saw it the first time. It was, maybe, June or a little later. ...A quiet day. I heard the stream. ...Bigger than it is today. When the warm weather comes on, the leaves rot away and the spring washes the basin out some. In the summer, it dries up, but the basin they made is still visible."

"You come by a lot to check on it?" asked Amin, but it was not a serious question and Charles did not answer. Instead, Charles was thinking about how low the spring was and whether that might be a bad indication about the size or presence of Pepper Falls. He clambered back up to the road and strode away with the others close behind.

Amin and Hemo felt an urge to survey the area around them, even knowing in advance they would not be surprised by anything they saw, but to see it all with a different perspective. The example from Charles was not to play at some game; he had not asked them to imagine they were walking with the Indians or the pioneers. They were to remove the perspective of their time, the inescapable background to every moment they had ever had.

An hour into the hike, Charles went to the side of the road and sat on a stone wall. He said it was time for a break and took out some canteen water for a quick drink. Amin and Hemo stood nearby, neither feeling tired enough from the easy terrain and pace to need a rest, but Charles asked them, more than offered, to take a seat on the wall, adding that he was not expecting another rest stop until another hour had passed. Amin felt good when he took the weight off his legs. Hemo sat but he did not rest. He had the sense it was time for something to happen.

Charles obliged his tacit appeal. "We're leaving the road here. At the farmstead."

"There's a farm here?" wondered Hemo aloud while Amin had virtually the same thought.

"Not now. There was one. This wall is not a natural thing, you know. And those old apple trees over there are in a row. It doesn't quite look like one 'cause some of 'em are missing, but you can see they used to be part of an orchard."

The three wandered among the apple trees. The ground below the trees was hard and stony. Hemo kicked at a few shrunken brown apple husks attesting to the species above them.

"Did they have a well or get their water from a spring like the one back there?" asked Amin.

"Good thought you have there. If we needed water, it would be good to look around here. Since someone built a house here, they must have had good water. There are some clues about what they were using and I think I can come up with a confident answer to your question. First off, they wouldn't have gotten water from a spring like that one we saw. It doesn't flow all year."

"Have you looked around already? Is the house still here?" Hemo thought an old house would be better to see than another spring. He was not ready to imagine living in old times, but he could imagine finding some artifact, not a valuable one, just a distinctive one that he could sit on the table beside his bed and feel he had been somewhere significant.

"Over there." Charles nodded vaguely to one side and started to walk that way. "But first, the matter of water... I doubt they dug a well. The remnants of house show it was a marginal affair. It doesn't look like they ever invested any more work than they needed and there's a creek a hundred yards from the house."

"Big detective!" Hemo snorted out. "You already knew they wouldn't need a well."

Charles smiled. "I haven't studied the place much. Maybe there's more than I noticed. Maybe they dug a root cellar or a spring house or a well. They put the house over there. I don't see anything that looks like a barn."

There was not much to see, not of the sort Hemo was hoping to find. The ruins of the house consisted mostly of stones that had been a fireplace and chimney and, 15 feet away, the stone steps to the door. On one side, partly buried in dry leaves, some unplaned planks with marks from an ancient saw mill rested on large stone blocks that had served as the foundation. From the front door, a path to the road could be visualized. Some trees had sprung up within the path, but an unnatural flat surface of constant width could be seen. Charles waved at it with his hand and his two companions understood what he what meant to show them. Amin got into the spirit of their exploration and mentioned that the age of the oldest tree in the path would give a minimum age for when the place had been abandoned. Hemo pushed away leaves to see if the outline of the house could be seen. He wondered why more planks and stones were not nearby. He would have been pleased to make some discovery or make some observation like Amin, but he found nothing worth mentioning. Charles wandered in a circle around the house and discovered a flat collection of rocks, ten feet square. He called the others over and brushed the leaves away.

"What do you think this was? Maybe the floor of a smokehouse?"

They all bent down to inspect his find. They looked for signs of fire on the stone but did not find any. The accumulation of moss and lichens might have hidden the sign, but none of them thought it appropriate to disturb the site to clean off the stones any more.

"I can't even guess what this thing was," admitted Hemo, "but it's goddam cool." He ran his hand gently over the rocks, not disturbing them, not feeling them in the sense of learning anything from his touch, but reaching out to contact the past and a legitimate mystery. He forgot about Charles and Amin, and looked at the walls of a smokehouse, built with rough-hewn logs standing grey, vertical and windowless. He smelled the fire and his mouth watered at the scent of ham.

Charles rolled his eyes toward Hemo to call Amin's attention to his silent reverie and Amin, ever courteous, nodded his recognition of Charles' signal and then sat on the heavy rectangular rock that had been the stoop to the house. He faced the trail to the road and looked relaxed as a field worker taking a break from a ghostly farm, inspiring Charles to see him as a psychic conjuring an image of the house behind him.

Charles leaned against the smokehouse and peered through the window of the main house. He felt his ownership of the farm, his muscles tired but strong from the work embodied in it. He saw in the house what remained to be done: digging the root cellar he had been thinking about earlier, running a track for water from someplace up the creek (more for watering the vegetable garden than for household convenience), constructing a roof over the woodpile which could be done in a single afternoon; some other fruit trees could be planted to go with the apples, cherries and plums; a patch of blackberries would care for itself once it got going... The images flowed easily since he knew this was where he had been born to be. His strongest form of identity was in the work of his hands. He forgave every flaw in what he made as long as its function was fulfilled and everything he made did function eventually. None of his plans included beautifying the place; it was inherently beautiful for being deep in the forest and made from his own wit and sinew.

He could hear someone inside the house and the sound warmed his heart more than the friendly, successful independence of the dream to this point. Through the window he could see a shape moving around, a shape he knew to be Natasha's and though he could scarcely see her features, lust stirred in him. He wanted her to come outside with him even though he sensed she would not see him in this peculiar state of mind. He did not want her to be cooking or sewing or some other traditional womanly thing; better if they were partners in a modern sense although the Natasha he knew would not have been very handy as a farming pioneer. She would have adjusted he figured. She would have had his full attention day in and day out. Is that what she had wanted from him? Was the farm abandoned because the wife wanted the conveniences and stimulations of the city? The fantasy was taking an uncomfortable direction and Charles slapped Hemo on the back of the head as he passed by, "Moving out!"

"All right, we've seen what there is to see. What's the answer? How old is this place?"

"Not old at all to someone who was born of a Greece at the roots of democracy, like you Hemo. Farms like this were spread throughout New England until improved transportation brought competition from the more efficient operations of the mid-West. I can't see the pattern here in this place, but much of this might have been open country at the end of the 19th Century, pasture and hay fields at least. Somebody from the university could probably read the stone walls all through this forest and say which were built first and what they enclosed."

"Can't you tell, Charles?" asked Amin.

"No way! I've seen a lot of walls but I've not looked at them too closely. That professor could say how long it took for the frost heaves and random movements of the world to knock a wall down to the state it is in. And he could see how old the lichens are on the surface. And look at how two walls connect to say which was here first. Wait, now that I think of it, I do know from the pattern what some of these walls enclosed. Come on over that rise with me and you will be able to say yourself."

Amin and Hemo followed closely to a small flat terrace overlooking the creek. Four relatively tall stone walls boxed in a few grave markers, two standing more or less upright and four others lying flat. They had been carved with names and dates, but were too worn to read clearly but for a few letters.

"Maybe a professor could tease some dates out of those," Charles suggested.

Hemo bent down on both knees, almost in an attitude of prayer. He put his face up close to one of the standing stones and touched it lightly with his fingers, but could not discern any more than he had seen in his first glance.

"Not you or me or Amin is going to be a professor so this will have to stay a mystery," he concluded.

"I have something better than this old farm to show you guys. Pepper Falls... We'll need another hour at least so let's get on." Charles was irritated by the obscurities of the place, irritated that he could not follow more of the clues, irritated that that more had not survived the years, irritated that his skills belonged in a time so remote it could not even be dated.

Chapter 6 - Pepper Falls

From here they did not follow the road or any trail. Charles knew the destination and did not care about the precise way of getting there. They had followed the ridge of a long hill when they were on the road and then they dropped off to the left of the ridge nearly down to the creek. There was a parallel, long ridge on the opposite side of the creek which they could reach by climbing east or perpendicular to the creek. Turning left at this ridge, north or northeast, depending on where they reached it, would take them to the head of a narrow valley, marked by a small but conspicuous rocky outcrop. Well down that valley lay a smaller valley coming in from the east and hidden in that one, far enough back from the main valley that no one ever went that way, was Pepper Falls.

The image of the terrain in Charles' brain was no more sophisticated than an outline of ridges and valleys, including a few on the periphery of the route to Pepper Falls. He knew this image along was not at all sufficient to find his way for it was hard to know where one stood in the network of low hills where trees obstructed any long views. He would need to peer through the branches to see if a low place continued down as a valley, to read the vegetation to see which rise was more likely to be the true ridge, to feel the distance traveled as a hint to where the next turn was due, and to return efficiently to the right direction when it was clear they had strayed from the plan.

First, they had to cross the creek. Charles had crossed it before but did not know of an easy crossing, not in the spring when the water was high. He knew there were some places worse than others, so he led along the creek while he looked so the first place that was good enough, someplace where they would not get wet above the knees. He saw a log jam that would let them scramble on top most of the way across but it did not look sturdy enough to lean a bridge on it reaching over the main channel. A little farther upstream, there was a wide gravelly bed. He studied it and asked his buddies to study it to see if there was any place too deep to traverse. Charles remembered crossing there in a drier season. They all agreed there was a place on this day, only a yard across, where a swift current had no visible bottom. They moved on. The discussion at the flooded ford let Amin and Hemo know they were not going to find a real bridge and might get wet on a day not warm enough for it to be a desirable thing. A promising pile-up of boulders was next examined.

"It must have been a hell of a flood that brought these together," Charles mentioned with admiration for the forces of nature. They could step or jump more or less securely across most of the crossing except for a gap of six feet or less. Charles looked to the landward and searched for a log to span this distance. He did not see one nearby, but there was an old tree with some shelf fungus declaring rot in its trunk so he mustered his small team to the task of knocking it down. He climbed as high as he could feel secure in the strength of the foothold and swayed back and forth while Amin and Hemo pushed and pulled at ground level. It seemed a fool's errand at first, but they found a rhythm that fit the tree and it started to rock more and more. Then the roots seemed to grab at a certain angle and their progress stalled. Charles called for a rest of 30 seconds. Amin and Hemo breathed heavily, leaning forward with their hands on their knees. Hemo felt it was his responsibility, as the strongest one, to get this tree out of the ground. He had faith that Charles had chosen it well, that it could be conquered and he was sure Charles was counting on him to make it happen. Then Charles reminded his team of how they had all pushed a car out of the snow by going forward and backward, using the momentum of the hole where the wheel was stuck to escape. He exhorted them to be firmer in their attack and when they began again, he swung away from the tree first on one side and then the other, like a flag whipped by the wind until the angle was suddenly more in one direction. He hung from the trunk by his hands and worked his way higher, improving the leverage of his weight while Amin and Hemo shouted and hung their weight on the trunk as it slowly lowered to the horizontal, landing Charles softly on his feet. The three worked together to right the tree and lean it in the opposite direction and then the roots pulled out of the ground and the tree was free. By the time they wrangled it over the boulders and across the gap, Charles was soaked to the thighs and all three were tired in their arms and panting more heavily than before. Charles used a long pole to steady himself as he crossed and then tossed it back for the others to use in turn.

"This will be the hardest few yards of the trip. It's all easy from here," Charles reassured them from his resting spot on the eastern shore. When they were all over, Charles raised the pole horizontally over his head and declared in an oratorical voice, "I dub thee the Hemo Crossing!"   All three understood this name was in recognition of Hemo's exertions that had been noisily conspicuous and, probably, essential to the task. Charles threw the pole with both hands into the creek. His two-handed style had not been very effective and the pole ended up with one end on the boulders and one in the water.   Then Charles waded again into the creek and pushed the tree off its nearer foundation. The gap flowed unbroken beneath the sky.   The bridge could be rebuilt relatively easily, but only from the opposite side.   The three watched the water run by, new water that had not seen them engineer a route over its course.   "It's called the 'Hemo Crossing', not the 'Hemo Bridge'," Charles reminded them.   Amin wondered why Charles had wrecked their return passage, but Hemo knew it was done to make the river more wild.

The next stretch was easier than crossing the creek, but it was not a return to the effortless trek along the road.   Charles led them directly up the hill without any switchbacks to ease the way.   The time they spent at the farm was not in his original calculations for the trip and he worried they would not get to the waterfall in time for a leisurely lunch.   The slope was steepest at the onset, where the creek had cut most recently.   They grabbed at small trees to help lift themselves forward and dug their boots into the soil to gain footholds, and still they sometimes slid back a few inches before getting set enough to carry their weight. As they gained elevation, the slope moderated to a safer angle, but not so much they could take a step without carefully balancing their weight against the potential to slide down. They had each traversed similar terrain many times and unconsciously leaned forward so they would fall to their knees if their foothold crumbled. For a ways, Amin followed in the tracks Charles was making and sometimes Hemo followed in Amin's tracks on the slope. They followed like this as a way to climb without looking up to see where to go. They could move more easily if they focused on the placement of each step rather than the direction of travel.

Amin may not have tired fastest, but he had the least ego invested in the climb and stopped to lean against a tree and survey what lay ahead. He knew it was not a competition, but it was a test, a test he could fail only by complaining about it.

Hemo staggered past him without speaking. He was pleased to be passing and he tried to breathe steadily while he was close to Amin and careful not to make any motion that could be considered as disrespectful. Then, when he was a few steps farther, he let his lungs suck all the air they could take in as he tried to make up the oxygen debt his vanity had just incurred.

Charles may or may not have been in the best shape of the three, but he had the advantage of seeing ahead and therefore knowing when the climb would end so he paced himself to get there with the last of his strength. And if he found he had not judged it quite right, he could change course to track along the contour to rest while in motion. They all knew a version of this unnamed game and each played it in his own way, each winning the version he was playing when they all lay on the grassy patch at the top of the slope, fifteen minutes from the creek. By lying there to recover, each admitted the climb had been strenuous and was humbled by this admission.

"Good day for it," said Charles, sitting up. "Not too hot." He looked at his pantlegs, still wet and covered in dirt. They would be fine once they dried out. He thought of taking off his wet socks, but did not want to delay any more. He stood up, adjusted his day pack, and stretched his legs and back. Fresh blood ran though his veins and he was strong again.

Although Charles had not been to this exact place before, he was sure they had arrived at a ridge and that it was very likely the right ridge. So he led them to the left, more or less northward.

At first, the growth on the ridge was sparse, probably because the weather was most severe here in the winter. As the ridgeline tended down, it fell below the surrounding hills and flattened to the sides, no longer having an obvious direction. Charles led around the densest growth and changed direction whenever he saw a relatively steep decline, trying to follow the ridge and trying to keep to the left of side of it, where he could find the neighboring valley. His searching glances and frequent stops to peer through the trees worried Amin who was beginning to think that Charles did not know the way. In fact, Charles was starting to think the same thing. And Hemo had no thought about the matter. He was content to follow and to deal later with whatever turned up as a result.

Charles considered climbing a tree to see farther, but a view suddenly opened up and he saw enough to decide they had reached the main valley he sought. He pointed to a rock, a small ordinary rock embedded in the dirt at his feet and claimed he recognized it and that it pointed to Pepper Falls.

"OK, Daniel Boone," said Hemo feeling educated for making an historical reference, one he doubted Amin would know. He wanted Amin to ask what he meant, but Amin was silent.

The going was easy as they slowly worked their way down and Charles felt more relaxed, seeing the valley lay before them. He was pretty sure it was the right valley. There was a brightness coming through the trees to the right although the sun was high in the sky more or less directly ahead. Charles tended toward the light until he could see it was due to a long, steep talus slope. "It's time for a break," he announced. "We'll settle in up there," and he gestured to the top of the slope. Neither Amin nor Hemo understood there was a talus slope nearby. Neither had a thought about why there was so much more light in one direction.

Amin wondered why they would start to climb up again and he suspected Charles was hiding the fact that he was lost and needed to look from a high place for some new sign of the way back. Hemo did not notice their march had changed direction because he was content to be a follower on this trip.

Five minutes later, Charles reached the top of the scree scar he had sensed from the side. The soil was thin on the steep rocky soil and populated with small, scrubby pines and stunted oaks. By grasping these trees for security, the three worked their way cautiously to a narrow ledge wide enough to support them seated side-by-side for lunch with a thrilling view. They each sat carefully but close to the edge. Charles took out a block of cheese he had sliced into three chunks and wrapped in plastic. He broke a baguette in three and handed a piece to each of his pals. They looked out on a wide valley bordered with long low hills. Leaves had not opened on all of the trees, but a green haze the color of buds about to burst had settled across the south-facing slope while a red haze of tiny maple blossoms covered the north slope. Small white globes of dogwood blooms showed thinly and distinctly through the branches of their taller neighbors.

"What the hell are you doing?" asked Amin of Hemo.

"What? Nothing. I'm eating lunch. The same goddam lunch he always gives us."

"It's a different cheese. I usually bring a softer cheese, like Havarti. I like it with dill, you know."

"But this is Swiss, right? It has the big holes."

"Right."

"That's probably the only cheese I know."

"You should not apologize for knowing something, Hemo. You know the variety of cheese. That does not make you effete."

"Fuck you, Mister Charles."

"My point illustrated."

"But what were you doing?" Amin asked again. "You were rocking back and forth like you were listening to music, but you have no headphones."

"I wasn't rocking. Oh, I know what you mean. I was trying to see it all in 3-D. It was like looking at a, like, huge wide-screen TV image. If I move my head to the side, I can see things move in front of other things. It's more 3-D."

"Hemo," Charles shook his head. "That is so sad. You have reality in front of you and you want to see an ultra-wide screen. Since it is a clear day, it's in high def too!"

"Fuck you all over!"

"I am just offering my sympathies. I can see you want to get in touch with reality. You want to see in 3-D. That's great."

Hemo understood the sympathy but he did not respond further. Amin looked across the scene, moving his head side to side.

"Hey Charles," he said, still rocking slightly," see those little trees? They have two kinds of nuts on them. Why is that?"

Charles saw where Amin was looking.   He went to the trees and collected a couple things. "This is an acorn," he explained. "This is the nut from an oak. We have lots of kinds of oaks and their acorns all look a little different. And this," he held out a rough, dark brown orb about twice the size of the acorn, "is a gall. A wasp lays an egg in the oak and the chemicals it plants makes the oak grow this ball to protect it." Charles took out his pocket knife and cut into the gall. "See inside? This is where the wasp larva grew. You can see the hole it made when it came out." And he handed another gall to Amin. Hemo leaned toward them but he could not quite see the gall and did not want to ask about it. Amin thanked Charles and rolled the gall around in his fingers.

A musical screech came to them from the scene.   Charles looked around intently. "They're mobbing that crow." But the explanation meant little to Hemo or Amin.

"What do you mean 'mobbing'?" Hemo asked on behalf of both. He felt left out of the gall story.

"You know, the little birds gang up on the big birds to chase 'em away. It's funny that it works. As far as I can tell, the little birds can't actually hurt the crow."

"I hear him but I can't see him. He's so loud he's got to be nearby."

"Look down, not up. He's flying below us. See him over there?" and Charles pointed to the crow.

"Oh wow! You can see the little ones flyin' at 'em!"

While they discussed the ritual confrontation floating before them, Charles searched for the dell where Pepper Falls would be if the water was flowing. He thought he could see it, the dell, not the falls, but could not see any landmark that might guide them there with certainty. The only omen that made him feel he could tell which little valley was the right one was the grey fog tucked into the upper reaches of the third notch away. It foretold moisture, of course, and it suggested the valley had seen little sunlight due to its steep sides. Together, those evidenced conditions for a cascade.

With no certain route, he decided to try to reach the falls from above. That way they would not need to backtrack on the way home. He had been above the falls before and could hope to recognize something. He stared at the scene while finishing his lunch and then handed out the second half of his baguette to Amin and finished the last of the water he had brought. Amin gave the bread to Hemo and Hemo thanked Amin and Charles before stuffing as much as he could into his mouth. "And thank you,

Hemo," Charles answered, "for making my load lighter for the walk back this afternoon."

"Do you know where we're going?" asked Amin. "You were looking awfully hard, like you were trying to find something hard to see."

"I absolutely know exactly where we're going, friends. I'm just not very sure where it is. That's OK, 'cause I know how to get there." Charles stood up and brushed the bread crumbs off his shirt. "We follow the ridge to the third small valley on the right, the one with the cloud in it." He pointed to the east and his two companions looked off along the ridge. The cloud was sharply edged where it was not sheltered by the hillsides and there was enough air movement to cut it off. Charles thought of the white napkins made of dewy spider webs that he saw scattered on the grass behind his house on summer mornings.

"I'm not sure what counts as a valley. Those are just small notches in the hillside. They don't go very far," Amin worried aloud.

"Yeah, I see the cloud. Right there, Amin." Hemo showed more faith in the vague plan. "You think it will still be there where we get that far?"

"It made it this far in the day and the day is cool, so yeah, I think it will be there. But it doesn't matter. We can find the third valley. From the ridge, those notches will be big enough when we reach them."

"Well, we don't even need to see ol' Pepper Falls if we get to walk inside the cloud. That would be cool all by itself!" Hemo further enthused.

"You're right. It doesn't matter. We'll see something. Just get us back before dark. Do you have that figured, Charles?"

"If you look hard at the lowest place over there," Charles indicated the direction with a slicing motion that defined a plane, "you may see the glint of a passing car from time to time. The road's not so far away." Charles had not wanted to mention the road. He preferred they would feel far from civilization, in time if not in miles. And then it would be a welcome surprise when they came upon it just as it seemed clear they were would be caught by the dusk. But Amin was worried and the afternoon would be harder for him if he were feeling insecure.

They climbed back to the ridge. Going directly, it was only ten minutes stiff hiking. It was not hard to follow the ridge to the northeast. The ridgeline was narrow here and the walking was easy. Exposure to the wind had dwarfed the trees and stunted the undergrowth. Eons of low growth, during which erosion had carried nutrients away, had impoverished the thin soil. Their boots did not rustle in leaves along the ridges. What leaves had fallen there in the autumn had long since blown away. This terrain held little moisture. The new crop of spring consisted of rocks pushed up by the frosts that still came nightly.

It was not much longer, no more than twenty minutes, before Charles led them over the lip of the ridge down a steep portion that briefly afforded a view of the route ahead. It was enough to rebuild his confidence in the route they were taking. "The falls'll be down this draw. We'll find the crease in the cut, and hope the water is flowing full and hearty."

His formula might have been too simple. The "crease in the cut" took them into a dense rhododendron thicket with blooms that seemed made of bright, shiny tissue paper, floppy and crinkled. The trunks of the low forest were gnarled like thick roots. They were narrow and flexible but very tough. They could not be pushed aside, but had to be traversed very consciously, placing each step so the boot rested on the ground rather than twisted against one of the trunks. It was merely one degree better than walking through a mangrove swamp, the point being granted for the dryer footwear among the rhodos. Charles usually went around a rhodo thicket, but he was afraid of losing track of the lowest part of the draw and he anticipated it would be only a few yards across. He soon wondered why he had that expectation. His companions grunted to show their displeasure at his route but did not go so far as to utter an actual syllable of complaint. Charles figured they were working on a clever jibe so he ought to prepare his own cutting retort. He did not understand their grunts were sincere expressions of their effort. They actually felt honored to be enclosed in the gentle, fragrant, ephemeral beauty of the plants but could neither admit nor deny their appreciation.

"Wait up!" Hemo called out, and Charles gave his full attention to the next words, expecting them to be well prepared. But Hemo was spontaneous and innocent. "This is getting cool. I can't see shit past where you're standing in front of me and Amin's standing behind me. We're in some kind of fog land."

"This is getting' weird," added Amin. "I didn't know you could have fog this late in the day. Unless maybe you're on the coast."

"It's not weird," Charles claimed. "It's just hard to get through. We'll be out of it in a minute. We may be moving slow but we're going straight to the falls."

"You know what would be really wicked cool?" Hemo asked. "Write this down. It'll be on Broadway someday. What if you filmed us high steppin' and twist walkin' through here and then erased the trees away? We'd look like dancers, modern dancers, Dance Theater of Harlem like, New Dance Theater of Hampshire. Maybe you could speed up the motion so we looked way agile! Doo, wop wop; doo wop, wop." Hemo keep singing his syllables to no particular tune.

"Be hard to set it to music 'cause we're all steppin' at a personal pace," Amin suggested.

"Didja hear Hemo's beat?" Charles wondered aloud. "Three to a bar. He's in a waltz. Me, I'm more of a foxtrotter when I'm cutting through the brush."

"I don't know much about local dances, but I'd say the foxtrot is for old farts. C'mon Charles, that's not your flavor! Back home we dance the tissint. It's for weddings. The man swipes a curved knife around and around the woman, closer and closer. She looks at his eyes the whole time and dances with him until he is on his knees in front of her. That dance moves. If I dance alone, I am thinking about the tissint in my dream. A dance needs to be hot. You don't know Moroccan customs? Maybe Latin: salsa maybe. What else do they have? Brazilians know how to dance and they don't need a partner for it." Amin contributed.

"Rhumba like this." Charles straddled a small bush and shimmied, mainly in his shoulders.

"I don't know how to rhumba or salsa, but I know for goddam sure, that's not either one of 'em." Hemo laughed.

"Shhhh," said Charles as he stopped his dance suddenly, staring ahead. He held one hand up to further quiet his companions. He squinted his eyes and leaned forward to see better what had caught his attention. He edged forward a little. His feet found their way safely through the confusion even without his attention. Maybe going slowly allowed his subconscious to feel the trunks and branches well enough to navigate and maybe it contained enough residual memory of the maze to carry him through the next few steps. Maybe he was just lucky not to get tangled. Charles was about to wave Hemo and Amin forward when he realized what he was seeing. "Damn! Forget it. It's nothing. See those shapes on the tree up there? I thought they were birds. They would have been big birds, not giants, but not songbirds. And to have so many roosting in the afternoon would be odd. But more than that, having them sit still while we were making all that noise would have been really odd. Who could sit still with Hemo in full song?

"Oh man," Hemo whispered. "I see 'em too. What the fuck are they? Wait, I see one's moving!"

"It's just leaves. Bunches of leaves hanging down. Oaks sometimes do that. It's a small oak tree."

"I love the fog, man!"

"Well, oak leaves mean we're out of the rhodos," Charles reminded them.

"Too bad. I was just getting my steps worked out. Gettin' a system; getting' a beat, you know? Let's go back this way so's I can do it better next time!" Hemo waggled his torso excessively as he emerged from the thicket.

"I hope you know," Amin said in a monotone, "the weirdest thing around here isn't the fog or the midget trees or the ghost birds. It's Hemo."

Hemo smiled broadly although no one was looking at him. He liked being outgoing and wished he felt relaxed enough to dance like a fool when he was at the bar trying to be good company for a woman.

Charles waited for the others to extract themselves entirely from the thicket. He stared appreciatively at the blooms and then turned back toward the falls. The signs were all positive: the sides of the dell rose more steeply on each side, the ground before him declined steadily, and, best of all, the leaves under his feet were soggy. He guessed there was a flow underneath them.

Within the next five minutes, they were past the fog; blue sky overhead. Small cliffs arose to the left of their track. Charles pointed to places where water flowed over the rocks although neither Hemo nor Amin knew what he was indicating. Charles was relieved to see the water build up. Within another five minutes, they were walking beside a small stream. It had emerged from under the leaves and hardly fit into a channel, but it had become strong enough to wash away whatever fell onto it.

"Spring," Charles soon noted. More water came from a small pool under a rock outcrop five feet high. It doubled the rill they were following. It was the only tributary he noticed though the stream continued to grow for the next five minutes of their hike. It was a legitimate stream at that point, bubbling in friendly fashion over smooth stones and pooling in places into small mirrors of the mossy rockface rising still higher on their left.

They had to walk on the right side of the stream because the water hew closely to the cliffs, but even on their side the footing was insecure. The bank rose steeply; the soil, where there was any, was soft and muddy, the rocks, loose.

And then Charles' heart jumped in his chest. He would have been embarrassed if his friends could know how happy he was to see the sky ahead shining through the branches nearly to ground level, indicating they were approaching the head of the cascade. He did not mind revealing that he liked the falls; he had brought them here after all; but he was open to ridicule, however good natured, to show how much pleasure he felt at the romantic scene they were about to witness, or to acknowledge he was not absolutely certain they were in the right place until he saw the space ahead.

He stopped walking. Hemo and Amin had been looking down as they progressed, wary of the footing. They both reached him and looked up to see why he stopped. Charles lifted his head enough to direct their attention forward. They looked without comment, aware they were getting somewhere. "Go ahead," said Charles to them both. He had not stood atop the falls before and anticipated it would be a grand sight, and it was a further gift to let them be there before him, to let them show it to him. He waited while they went the last fifty yards and then, when he saw them stop, he went on to join them. "Whatta you got?" he asked as he got close.

Neither of them turned to respond. "Unfuckin'believable!" answered Hemo under his breath.

The stream dropped into an open chasm as if it just ended in space. They had to climb around to the side to see the falls clearly. After several drops, each larger than the previous one, it landed in a deep pool nearly hidden by rock and fern and laurel, the latter either pink or more mature white. A deep drone came back to their ears from the pool thirty feet below.

"See how the water stays tight up at the top?" asked Amin. "It's like it sticks together. It doesn't splash all over. But down at the bottom, it's just mist when it's falling the last bit."

"I wonder if that doesn't depend on the day?" asked Charles. "If there's more water or less water, it might not look like that."

"But you've been here before. What was it like then?" asked Hemo.

"Well, I never stood on the top before. And I don't remember seeing the water look so tight. I think I would have noticed that sound it's making. Don't you think all the noise is coming from the top?"

Amin sat on the ledge, off to the side from the water, at a place where he could rest his feet on a small lower ledge.

Hemo watched Amin settle in cautiously and then picked a place as close as possible to the stream. He wanted to be near enough to put his hand in the water, but the stream was sunken below any place to sit comfortably. Getting close enough for his hand to reach in would have been perilous. He let his legs hang over the edge. He was not comfortable either because of the cold hard rock or because he felt insecure with the open volume of empty space in front of him, but he felt he belonged just there; it was his place in the scene. He wished there were a photographer. Lacking one, he decided to sit there as long as the others were looking at him, imprinting the image of him in their brains.

Charles sided with Hemo in the uncomfortable pleasure of acrophobia. He stood between his two partners and leaned into the space slightly, not enough to fall, but enough to minimize the view of the ground at his feet. From their vantage point, the flowers were clearly different from the large rhododendrons, but the balls of laurel blossoms were comparable in size and gave the same impression of excessive display, even while the individual cups that made up the inflorescence could not be distinguished. They all looked into the well, each with a unique view of what lay below them.

Charles wondered how the scene changed over the year; how brilliant it would be if the water were flowing full when the winter hit this mountain and froze some version of the cascade and the broad-leaved bushes held full shares of soft snow, forming bulbous shapes to meet the imagination, like clouds on a warm day; how fine it would be to discover the day of the year and the time of the day when the sun squeezed into the notch in the hillside and lit the spray from the sides of the slim torrent, giving another dimension to its movement; how calming it would be to come here on the hottest day of summer, hiking fast and alone, when the stream had reduced to a trickle over the cliff where he could dip his head and cool back to a milder state; how wonderful it was that there was no stream and no waterfall in mid-summer and into the fall when the forest endured the most intense invasion of hikers and hunters such that there was no trail to and around the falls, little prospect of finding any interloper, and no official name to the place he had introduced to his friends as Pepper Falls.

Hemo pictured himself jumping off the jagged rocks where he was sitting, not head first because he would surely hit the bottom but a precisely aimed leap full of motion and coordination, the dive boys show to each other rather than one designed for female eyes. And then he imagined camping in a tent in view of the falls amid autumnal color with the woman he had met a couple weeks before at a bar, just as she was leaving, who looked healthy more than packaged up for sex, and who answered his greeting with an open smile and a confident look into his face that had come so easily she surely liked the look he was giving out at that moment. And he envisioned trekking through the wilderness in the days before everything was on a map

and there could be surprises around the bend, carrying
a musket, maybe, for the bears and puma, if there were
ever big cats in these woods, not for Indians because he
would have been the type to get along with them, to
tread lightly on their landscape and keep their secrets,
secrets they would have allowed him to know after they
knew him enough to trust him, secrets about how to
survive and how to carve small objects in the image of
their gods of nature and how to tell what the weather
would be just looking at the signs around them, and the
original and real names for the mountains, streams,
valleys, flowers, animals and other notable parts of the
landscape.

Amin projected coming to the falls with a series
of women, testing them to see who is the right one: the
one who keeps up with his pace while hiking in but
does not think a faster pace would have been better;
the one who notices the beauty of the place and credits
him with bringing her to it; the one who says little about
the sights because she is entertaining him with
imaginative stories from her childhood, stories that
reveal her to have been unprivileged except for being
well loved by her parents, to have been desired by the
boys without believing that was an accomplishment, to
have learned practical things, not so much classroom
things, things like how to use the wild and domestic
plants and fungi and animal parts that would serve her
and him well when they built their cabin and barn and

smokehouse by the river, and planted their orchard and garden.

Charles looked for a way down to the gorge and decided it would be a difficult climb unless they went wide around the cut in the hillside and backtracked. The sight had been seen and it was past time to be getting back home. The stream fitted into a narrow cut that was rarely exposed to sun and the shadows that darkened the slopes above their height made the late hour conspicuous. He marched the small band down to the valley without a look back and no one spoke for three-quarters of an hour until they could see the road forming an unnatural straight, horizontal break in the tangle of branches ahead of them.

"How far it by road back to town?" asked Amin.

"I'm not sure exactly where we are. I'd say it's five or six miles from here. We'll see how long it takes for a neighbor to give us a lift, eh?"

The tradition of hitchhiking has fallen away in America, but not so far that people do not understand what it means to hold out a thumb while walking a country road. It was not long before someone who did not care about current styles or who did not know the modern status of hitching a ride, stopped his pick-up and offered the three a seat in the bed. He was not such an old-fashioned fool as to let strangers into the cab with himself.

Chapter 7 - Charles New Project

The ride took them within a mile of Charles' house. They were lucky to get that close since no major roads came any closer. It was not especially late in the day when they jumped out of the back of the truck and thanked the driver, but it felt late since it was already dark and the cold air blowing across the back of the truck made it feel like winter again. Charles took out Amin's jacket which he had picked up in the morning and gave it to Hemo. "Sorry I forgot when we got in the back of that truck that I brought this." Hemo was shivering. He grunted his appreciation. Charles was surprised Hemo took the vest and realized he must really be cold.

The mile to Charles' house was neither pleasant nor unpleasant. Their legs were tired from the hike, but they were young legs and strong enough to handle the day. They were stiff from the cold ride, but quickly warmed up when they began to walk again. The three did not speak; the darkness of the country road allowed each his privacy. They felt no need for chatter. When they neared the houses, a light rain was beginning. Charles suggested they all take Amin's pick-up out to Charles' van and then they could all finish up a good day with dinner at the diner. "That's what it was, right Hemo? A good day, even if you didn't get laid?" Hemo suspected he was being mocked, but the question was mildly respectful since it implied he did get laid on some good days, consistent with the reputation he wanted to own. While he ruminated on this point, Charles shouted "Shotgun" so he could sit by the window on the ride out to the van.

Amin started up his truck and asked Charles as he bounced along the road they had just walked, "You said you were going make some changes, you know, since Natasha left, but you didn't mention anything all day. Do you have a plan?"

"Not a plan for getting her back. She's gone. In her head, there is no coming back and in my head, she shouldn't come back. She's right that I'm not right for her. Except for that, she'd be perfect for me. And I don't have a plan to replace her either. You may not know it, but finding a woman is not that easy. I never found one by following a plan anyway. I'll drift along and see what turns up."

"But you said you were making changes..."

"Changes? Sure. I'm trying to find a way to make money. What I've been doin' doesn't add up to much. I like the work, most of the time, but I'm too slow to get rich at it."

"You need to specialize, man" Hemo interjected. "You do some of everything so you never fine tune the job. There's always ways to get it done faster, more efficiently, but you need experience; experience with the specific job, I mean. Like at my job, I know better than that fuckin' Oscar, my boss, you know, better than him how to do the stupid shit I do. He should listen to me. It would be to his advantage."

"You're right both ways, Hemo. I should specialize and Oscar ought to take advantage of your thinking while you're working. If the world wants efficiency, and sometimes it does, someday Oscar will be working for you. But I like running my own small operation and that means I can't specialize. I don't want some Oscar getting in the way. I earn my pittance! But let me say I do have a plan. I have been fixing other people's stuff, which believe me does not pay much, so I'm going to fix up something I own. I'm lookin' at that old place on Orchard Street. Have you been down there?"

"Orchard? Don't know it" Amin answered while Hemo shook his head in the negative.

"Yeah, you've been there. It's along the river, but up above it enough it won't get wet in the spring. You go off Route 105, you know."

"Orchard! Sure. It's gotta be a mile from 105 down to the river though," Hemo remembered.

"You mean that skinny road on the left about three miles north of town?" Amin asked.

"Yeah, yeah. You've been down to the river that way. We went there last summer."

"I know it, but I don't know the house."

"I know it. Two stories; porch across the front; used to be white. It's beat down. Can you save it?" Hemo was pleased he could name the place.

"Yeah, I looked at it close," Charles explained. "The frame is solid. The layout is pretty nice. The roof's no good. I would have to replace the roof and the siding, but the roof is good enough to protect it up to now. I priced up what it would take to get it in shape. I counted the cost of my labor. I don't want to pretend I have a lot of free time to do it. It will be a stretch. And then I can move in by the end of summer and start saving on my rent. I can do the interior in small pieces over the next year and sell the place for a good profit. I like trying different..."

"No," Hemo interrupted. 'You don't want that fucking place. You know who owned it?"

"Sure, I looked it up in the town hall. It belonged to an old man. His daughter moved him to a rest home two years ago. He died and now she owns it with her brother."

"The old man worked for Robbie. Robbie owns that house, no matter what the courthouse says. Least he owns it if it's worth anything."

"Robbie? Who's he? You know him?" Charles had heard the name only one place. It had been repeated on that rainy morning on the river, one of the few clear words he had heard. It was a common sounding name, but Charles had never met anyone who called himself "Robbie." He decided that morning he did not want to meet Robbie, but he had not heard enough that morning to change his life.

"You know. He's the local sleezeball. You don't wanna know him," explained Hemo.

"I heard of him," added Amin. "He's the guy can get you whatever you want if you got the bucks."

"Well, he's not the owner of record, and this place is virtually abandoned. I've got a plan."

"I'm just saying, since you's such an innocent son of a bitch, you don't want any connection to Robbie. If he turns up, give him what he wants and walk away."

"Yeah, OK. I won't try to push around any gangsters who might retain an interest in this dump I want to renovate."

It was late for dinner when they finally made it to the diner, but no one cared. In fact, it was good for Charles and Hemo, who preferred not to recall they had nothing better to do in the evening than eat in a cheap diner. They would all sleep well that night.

Charles did not like the connection to the disreputable Robbie, but he did not think Hemo's rumor and speculation were enough to force a change in his plan. He bought the old house from the out-of-state daughter without the benefit of a real estate agent. He felt like a tycoon to call her up, make her an offer, and convince her she would not do better by going through conventional channels.

He began by moving to the new project all the lumber and hardware he had accumulated in his shed over the years. He always used new parts on repair jobs so he had saved this stuff for his own venture when it came along. He guessed the salvaged items would save him a thousand dollars: cabinet knobs in turned wood or cheap metal, switchplate covers, ceiling lights, outlets and their boxes, hinges... He had enough hinges to replace all the doors. A close survey of the house had shown him the doors needed replacing including their hinges. It would mean hanging the doors on the existing jambs rather than buying door jambs with the doors already hung. It was an example of Hemo's point that he was slower than a specialist. Any other builder would save the labor by buying the door-jamb combo. But it was also an example of his plan to make money. His labor would be hourly inefficient, but he would be selling more of it and making more money. At this stage in his vision, he wanted more money, not easier money.

It was exciting to see the house progress, and tempting to substitute work on it for work on his regular type of client, but he forced himself to take as many regular jobs as he would normally have. The house he was rebuilding was only for open time. That way he did not need to worry whether the rate of return on his time was competitive. This left him with no time for hikes, or dinners with friends, or meeting new women.

The house changed quickly while he was in the stage of tearing out walls and other features he did not want. Then it slowed down as he focused on making it weatherproof. And then it was time to start building up the new house.

One week he was busy with regular jobs and let a couple evenings go by without work on his project house. When Saturday came around, he took his morning walk and loved the early heat of the day so much he thought he ought to get away on a solitary hike somewhere. If he hurried, he could drive to the coast and take a mailboat out to an island. Summer had come and was going on without his taking any advantage of it. During his shower, he thought through whatever he would need to do. First, he would look up the mailboat schedule on the internet. He would stop in the supermarket to buy something quick to take with him for lunch and something for breakfast in the van while he drove; probably bread and cheese for lunch. He should fill up his canteen before he left, he reminded himself. Water was the cheapest drink and just plain water always tasted good when he was hiking. He imagined lying on a rocky beach, the sun upon him but not too hot because of the ocean air, no one in sight or earshot, washing down a baguette with fresh water while looking over the salt sea. He would pack his camera too. When he went alone, taking pictures was good company.

But when he was toweling off, he changed his mind. The isle was a siren taking him from his true course, getting back to the house. He knew his natural indolence and fought it with a scheduled routine, and that schedule called for him to take every chance to work on the house. He had nearly slipped but a whole day away would gouge a hole in his plan, getting him out of the habit and letting each small demand eat up his free time until the house was only a long-term dream. He needed to feel again the inspiration his first weeks on the project had brought, back when he could see a difference every time he went there. He called up Hemo...

"Hemo! What d'ya say?"

"Who the hell is this? It sounds like Charles but it can't be Charles. I heard he fuckin' left the planet a month or two back."

"Work, work, work, my man. That's all there is."

"Sure, I believe you. What's her name and where did you meet her?"

"That's a good idea. I should name the damn house. You have any suggestions?"

"How 'bout 'Natasha'?"

"Not funny. Listen, man, you busy today?"

"It's Saturday."

"Want to make some money?"

"I need more money than anything legal would bring in."

"What do you make working for Oscar? You still with him?"

"Now I gotta say out loud that I'm still with Oscar? Why would you do that to me? There is nothing less I want to say."

"What does that prick pay you?"

"Fifteen bucks an hour."

"It's more than I average, counting in all the time I spend getting jobs, planning jobs, buying parts, travel and all that. I'll pay you twenty an hour if you work on my place today."

"What am I? You don't pay me. I'd be glad to help you out. Like I said, it's Saturday."

"It's not helping me. It's helping my business. This is just a business proposition. Twenty bucks an hour. I'll throw in lunch."

"I know what you think lunch is."

"So bring your own peanut butter and jelly."

"No bread and cheese is OK. It's just predictable."

"I'm out of caviar. If you stop at Piggly Wiggly on the way out to the house, I'll compensate you for it."

"We don't have Piggly Wiggly in this state. No cheese with crap in it, like pimentos or peppers or that stuff they put in spumoni."

"You know where it is, right?"

"First I've got to get out of bed. Shit, shower and shave."

"Shave? On a Saturday?"

"I don't have that peach fuzz like some people in this conversation. If I let my beard go a day without cutting it back, it gets out of hand."

"I'm on my way out there now. I'll start the clock whenever you show up."

They met less than an hour later at the house. Charles had parked his van close to the front door where it could serve as his oversized tool chest. It was a pleasure for him to have all the tools accessible. Like a typical handyman, he was constantly refining how he arranged them to make each of them easy to find. He did not make toolracks with a furniture-maker's finesse, an architect's coordination, or a clock-maker's cleverness, but with a handyman's practicality, yet he appreciated finesse, coordination and cleverness— they just did not claim priority in his van.

Hemo drove in as Charles was making a pile of tools for the job. He was not sure what he was going to do next until he starting taking out the tools. His small spade had fallen on top of his tool belt so he had to move it, and held it for a moment to think of a way to hang it up, and realized this would be a good day to take on a part of the project he had been avoiding because it was pure work, but that is exactly where Hemo would be good.

"Hey there Hemo, my man. I trust my call did not wake you up too early for the weekend!"

"Hey fucker, I had to get up anyway to answer the phone."

"Language, my man! Do you eat with that mouth?"

"Sorry. I forgot your workplace had ethical standards."

"I do not challenge your ethics Hemo. I applaud your full-blooded integrity. But you need to tone down your profanity in front of the callow members of the staff around here."

"At twenty an hour, you call the job, the style, the language and any other goddam thing you want."

"Yep, that's how it ought to be. Listen, I've got the place fixed up to be safe and solid. Now I need to make it worth buying at a premium price. Don't you love this spot? It ought to bring a price."

"It's pretty nice here. Maybe you can get a fisherman. He could throw a line out from the porch."

"I see a family having lunch on the porch to the sound of the rushing waters in spring."

"Or the hum of blackflies in the summer... And by the way, did you ever work out the ownership of this project with Robbie?"

"The subject never came up with anyone but you, Hemo."

"Just don't make it so beautiful he notices."

"I expect a subtle, modest, family-size personal beauty. Nothing a rural gangster would want."

"He only wants the money."

"I wish it would be enough to interest this Robbie."

"What are we doin' today?

"Hard work, I'm afraid. I want to drop the basement floor down about two feet. Then I can pour a concrete floor and finish out the basement with an eight-foot ceiling."

"Eight feet is not luxury class."

"Right you are. Just a modest height. It will be good enough for a family room and some quality storage space. I think we've got easy soil, just silt from the floods of the last million years; no bedrock. I did a couple test holes a few weeks ago..."

"Where we gonna dump it?"

"I don't have that figured exactly. There's a lot of slope on the back, looking over the river. Maybe I should put in a retaining wall and build out a patio area." Charles waved to Hemo to follow him around the house to look over the grade and he glanced at his watch inconspicuously, calculating Hemo had already been at the site for five minutes. He did not rush through the discussion of where to put the dirt they dug out. Hemo was no landscape architect, but Charles needed to think out the plan and he did not want to disrespect his buddy to save a few dollars in his wage. "I'll show you around inside when you're off the clock."

"I get it, Oscar Junior. Let's dig!"

They went down the rough steps to reach the basement with their shovels, a pick-mattock, and a wheelbarrow.

"Sorry I didn't think of it on the phone. Did you bring some gloves?"

"You're talkin' to a pro, man. I brought the gloves, the callouses, the blisters, and the big, aching muscles that deserve a twenty per hour workday."

The basement was cool, dark, humid, and cramped; neither man could safely stand up straight. In a minute, their eyes adjusted enough to see the whole space clearly. There were narrow windows all around the perimeter, not large enough to make it bright, but good enough for work.

"We'll start by digging out a ramp on this side. Then we can run the wheelbarrow up the ramp after that."

Charles worked on the one side of the exit door while Hemo worked on the other. Charles first dug out a trench across the base of the ramp, at the level of the final floor. He had prepared a "story pole," a stick one inch by two inches, eight and a half feet long with a mark at two inches and six inches, indicating where the top of the gravel and the top of the concrete would eventually be. He would hold the pole to the ceiling to test whether the floor level had been reached. The soil was clear, as Charles had hoped. Meanwhile Hemo labored like a diesel machine, guessing how deep to make his trench. Charles would make another story pole for him next time they were digging.

They did not talk to each other, respecting the job, the business, but Charles could hear Hemo working steadily and was chagrined at his apparent pace. Chares shifted to building the ramp while Hemo used the story pole to level out area he had dug. The ramp was their temporary goal and they both watched it take form, not racing, not competing, but aware of each others' efforts until Charles christened the ramp with a sudden sprint up it into the light and flopped onto the ground.

"Mercy, mercy, John Henry" he called out. "Let a poor sinner rest. Break out the water! No, no, don't get it! Sit yourself down. Management will get it," and he jumped up and with the last of his strength sprinted to the front of the house to get the jug of ice water. He walked back to Hemo slowly, his breath heaving from his short run, and then collapsed beside him, landing on dried leaves although Hemo was lying on the side of the dirt pile. Charles looked at him pointedly and at the dirt around him.

"It's cooler," said Hemo.

Charles peeled a paper cup off the stack and filled it with water for Hemo. Then he filled another for himself. He took the first cup back from Hemo and filled it again and then handed him an apple. "Need to stoke the engine with a little sugar."

They sat side-by-side for ten minutes crunching apples. Charles ate his down to a spindly skeleton of seeds and the shell around them. He showed the remnant to Hemo and tossed it aside. Hemo held up what remained of his core and popped it into his mouth, consuming it completely. "We're about forty bucks into the day and the boss is already beat... Once this sugar kicks in, we'll try going another forty bucks and then we'll have lunch. OK for you?'

"Can't cool down too much. It'll be hard to get going again. Up and at 'em, management." Hemo stood up and tapped Charles with his toe.

Charles found a plank twelve feet long and laid it on the ramp as a track for the wheelbarrow. "The only goal for the day is to go as long as we feel like going. The most we would do is open the floor to within a foot of the perimeter. I don't want to get any closer in case it would weaken the existing foundation. Then I'll put in a footer in each corner and mid-point of each wall for the new supports. After I pour the new floor, I'll build a block wall and have a regular basement that can be finished into a den for middle Americans. You see the picture?"

"It's really beautiful. You've got a vision. You're going to make it real. How do you know how to do all this anyway?"

"I don't know how to do it. I am just making it up."

"What if the wall slides when we get the floor dug close to it? Is the house gonna fall on us."

"Probably not. What do you think?"

"Doesn't look like it."

"Better get a new foundation in place before there's a big rain."

"It won't rain much this time of the year."

"Yeah. Probably not. Not today anyway."

The process did not work quite as Charles had envisioned. A wheelbarrow of dirt was too heavy to push up the ramp so he tied a rope to the axle and they took turns being the pusher or the puller on the short lift to the outside. Hemo worked his shovel steadily over the afternoon hours, showing no decline as the sun fell behind the leafy trees. The official sunset was still more than an hour away on this long summer day, but Charles was looking for an excuse to end the workday. He monitored the shadows on the house and when the house was covered, he declared the basement too dark to continue working. Hemo harrumphed the weak excuse. He was satisfied he had been right that it had not rained through the rest of the day and that the house had not fallen upon the two workers.

"I'll leave the wheelbarrow in the basement, but we'll pack the shovels in the van. I don't have an exact place for them yet; just throw 'em in the back."

"You can't lock up the place with that hole in the side going into our ramp."

"Damn right. I knew it would be open for a while so I don't have anything stored in the house yet; no tools, no new lumber, just old ssalvage. Anyone wants this crummy wheelbarrow is a sorry son of a bitch and welcome to it."

"What about liability? Some little dude rummages around looking for something or some drug freak thinks it's a place to hide out and starts a fire or the foundation collapses where we weakened it, and then his mama sues you for letting him hurt himself...."

"Kind of you to be thinking of this for me. I gotta admit, you have a good point. I should keep the place secure. I have insurance, but it won't cover me if I am negligent. Presumably letting someone use my house for a drug overdose without breaking in might well constitute negligence. I'll just take a risk until I get to a point where I can lock it up again. You see, this is where it is good that Natasha is not with me anymore. I can take a risk with my assets. The worst a lawsuit could do would be to bankrupt me. That's not so much to lose, is it? You know, just start over. I still have my youth."

"Bankrupt takes away your reputation with the banks. You want to be an independent operator, man? You need those banks."

"The banks haven't done me any good yet. If Natasha were watching, I could not take the risk on myself. If she were inside my economy, I could not take the risk on ourselves. But it's just me. What the hell; a few days. I don't think there is a real danger to this place, but if you want to send out some idiot to get himself injured so he can sue me for my tool chest, ten-year old van, and the deed to a dangerous property by the river, go for it."

"Alright, thanks for the opportunity. There'll be no hard feelings, right? First thing, though, I need a shower read bad."

"I need a shower and a long night sleep. Maybe I'll take Sunday off too."

"You'll let me sleep late tomorrow?"

"I won't have my phone on and I won't answer the door until hunger drives me from the bed."

"So what time are you cooking breakfast for your employees?"

"I may just go for some ice cream tonight and could go for a big breakfast. Wanna meet at the diner in the morning?"

"Not before ten, boss."

"OK, not later than ten either; at the diner. I'll bring your paycheck. Damn good work today, buddy."

Charles stopped at a gas station to fill up the van and then washed up as well as possible in the rest room to make himself presentable enough to buy a dish of ice cream in the general store. As it turned out, there were no tourists in the store anyway. He was not concerned that the clerks would look critically at a local lad in work clothes late on Saturday, as long as he was not tracking mud onto their worn wooden floors. The sandwiches listed and described on the chalkboard behind the glass case tempted Charles to eat something more substantial than he planned, but when he thought of the effort required to chew through the heavy bread they used, he went back to his ice cream idea. His options were in a row of cardboard tubs in the glass freezer, separated by a glass wall from the salads. A salad would not require much effort to eat and would be better for him, he supposed. He listened to the rising ache in his muscles and decided the calories were the right thing. He ordered a large cup, three scoops, of pistachio with fudge on top. That was always his mother's choice in ice cream. She would have had whipped cream too, but he thought that too fru-fru.

The woman who scooped up his ice cream was about his age and desirable as all women are desirable when they meet certain minimum standards and smile back at the customers. He nodded in a way he thought communicated his appreciation of her as much as the ice cream, but it was an insincere nod, only a courtesy. He really wanted the ice cream and some quiet time to consume it. There were several rocking chairs on the porch outside the shop. He sat in one and tried rocking. It made him feel antiquarian so he stopped and leaned forward to take his first spoonful. The cool sweetness was perfect for the moment. He let his weight go back while the lump melted in his mouth and the cream slid down his throat. In that posture, he could not see into the cup as he spooned out the pistachios, but his filthy clothes caused him no worry about spillage and he slowly, thoughtlessly worked his way through the rest of his dinner. The sweat in his armpits dried to a salty crust and he returned to the temperature of the air around him. The air was cooling with the declining sun and a fine day drew to a close.

Back in his house, he turned on the shower and laid out his summer pajamas, loose shorts and a shirt in a plaid pattern, while waiting for the hot water to work its way to the bathroom. It was not a long distance from the hot water heater, but he had such low water pressure, it could take several minutes for the temperature in the shower to stabilize. He moved the

TV into the bedroom in the evening so he would not need to get up from the sofa after he fell asleep. He stood in the shower, leaning against the wall so warm water poured over his head. He remembered he used to sit in a hot tub to relax his muscles although it had been some years since he had done so. That was too fru-fru too.

When he turned off the water, he thought he heard a toonk sound in the house. He could not think of how the plumbing could make such a sound. The best idea he had was that the water heater tank had broken somehow with the change in water pressure. He rushed to dry himself so he could check on it quickly, before a flood damaged whatever he was storing in the basement. His evening plan was disturbed but not yet ruined. The sound might have been a bird crashing into a window, an alternative Charles did not actively wish to be true if it would mean harming the bird. He stepped into the hallway fully naked on his way to the bedroom where his PJs awaited. Before he went through the bedroom door, a movement in his peripheral vision caused him to suddenly turn to his right. Two men stood in his living room, both smiling broadly.

"You are Charles?" one asked.

"Yes, I am. Who are you?" he asked back.

"Don't matter, not to you. We're just here to ask if you found anything in that old house that don't belong to you."

"You mean the house I am rebuilding on Orchard Street?"

"Yep. Orchard Street."

"I bought the house, so I guess it belongs to me. I didn't find a damn thing worth anything inside it. It's going to take a big investment of time and materials to make it pay off for me. But why would you ask? It's been empty for a year."

"Do you know who Robbie is?"

"I don't know anyone named that but I heard there is someone around here called 'Robbie'."

"Well, Robbie left something with the old man who lived there and he never got it back."

"There was nothin' when I got to the place." Charles shook his head slowly, not sure if it was bad acting or if it was a genuine expression of his negative answer to their interests. "You or Robbie can go look inside if you want. It's not even locked. There's a opening in back where we dug out the basement to get some headroom. Don't sue me if you get hurt. There're nails sticking down from the ceiling and who-knows-what on the floor."

"You tear down the walls yet?"

"Like I said, go look at it any time. The walls were all tore up before I ever got there. I took some out. The ones left in are structurally sound, I think, but the lathing was ripped open all over the place. It's mostly piled out back now. I 'll get a dumpster one of these days."

"You tell us if anything odd shows up, right?"

"I work for my return. I don't want anything I didn't earn. Really. I don't need any more than I earn. I'd like my girlfriend back, but I don't need much more and I sure don't steal another man's stuff. No matter what it is. If I find something other than the garbage and hard work I found so far, I'll report it. Tell you what, I'll report it to Robbie just 'cause I also don't want any trouble. You have a phone number or something for me to call?"

The two men were either satisfied by his answers or simply could not devise any further questions or threats. One who had been talking mumbled something more and put a small card on the kitchen table, which he could reach from where he was standing.

"Next time, just knock on the front door. I'll open it if I'm home."

After they left, Charles turned on the lights and saw that they had broken the window beside his front door, and gone through all the cabinets and drawers. They had not been neat about it. He nearly ran to the door and called them back so they would look in the bathroom too, but he let them go. If they were satisfied with their search, he would not try to change their minds. Fixing the window would be a nuisance, but he was not concerned about the rest of the mess. He felt a satisfaction in his freedom from possessions. If he had thought about it more deeply, he would have realized

he was not entirely free from valued possessions,
although his rented house, worn-out clothing, cheap
kitchenware, and shabby furnishings were of little worth
to him or anyone else. If his tools had been damaged,
he would have felt personally injured.

Chapter 8 - The Project Takes a Turn

Charles did not work all day Sunday, not on a paid job, not at his riverside house, not in the rented house where he lived, and not on the home of a friend. His breakfast with Hemo reminded him he had been ignoring his friends. Losing Natasha had made him question the role of social contact. He was willing to let it go for a time and use the energy for his business. He had thought his resolve referred to social contact with a woman, that he was giving up sex and whatever company only a woman provides, and had not realized he was hardly doing anything with anyone. Seeing Hemo, he was amused to see that Hemo had missed him. And he recognized he had missed seeing Hemo and other friends. But his time with Hemo was even more notable for its impact on his basement. They had not dug it out entirely, but the final shape of it could be seen. The full-sized, finished basement would be a huge upgrade to the house. It added, he guessed, $40,000 to the final value and he would be spending less than $15,000 to build it. ...Plus his own labor, of course. This was worth putting off one's buddies for a few months. The idea of getting back in touch with friends more actively or doing other leisure things had formed in his mind although he was not entirely convinced it was best. Ever since he realized back in first grade that there was no school between June and September, summer represented the most precious time of year. There were places to see and things to do that he was also missing on warm days in New England. So for one Sunday, he did nothing productive and thought constantly about how this was not going to break his pattern of progress. Later, when he thought back briefly to this day, he could not recall one thing more about it than this resolve to do nothing.

Thursday was his next day free from commitments and even then he had only half the day. The morning task required cutting some boards to length and then notching them to fit into the space under a window. He was building a box over a client's radiator. There was nothing he could do on the project that was quiet and he had promised the family where he was working not to start making noise before 7:30. That was when the kids were supposed to leave for day camp. Charles could not see why it was necessary for the kids to have a quiet house during their cereal. Most of his customers came from a social tier above his own but he adjusted to their idiosyncrasies; he got to the house early and hung around conspicuously, hoping one of the parents would suggest that he get started. They ignored him and he turned on the saw at exactly 7:30 even though the kids had not left the house yet. They were still in the kitchen, but Charles did not care. He had formal permission to proceed. He had the radiator cover cut, built, sanded, and primed before noon and taped a sign saying "wet paint" over it as his final professional act for the day.

He skipped lunch except for a drink and some kind of sticky nut bar that he bought at a gas station. By 12:30 he was parking the van outside the river-house.

With a thought to Hemo's curse, he walked around the house the long way looking for any sign of a stranger's entry. At last he came to the gaping hole into the house where the ramp had been built. The area in front of the opening was covered by the dirt he and Hemo had brought out. He inspected the area for footprints and could see only the ones they had left behind on Saturday. Relieved that no unlikely disaster had taken place, he completed his circuit of the house, returning to the van to get a shovel, posthole digger, his gloves, and some adhesive tape. The blisters from Saturday did not hurt any more, but he could not keep digging if he tore up his hands anew. He taped around the fingers that had blisters and wrapped a band across the palm of each hand. The Saturday experience was good for showing exactly what parts of his hands were vulnerable in this task with these gloves.

Inside the cool basement, he studied the sides of the room and visualized how they would look when completed. He decided to begin shaping by cutting into the soil bank where he would put the new foundation supports. He had no engineering background but was confident in his seat-of-the-pants assessment of what support was needed; he figured six piers would be enough. He would dig six footers and build six columns of concrete block, wedged to support the basement ceiling, that is, to support the whole house. He calculated how long it would take. There ought to be enough light left in the day to get them all dug if he did not hit any rock.

As he was filling the wheelbarrow for the first load, he suddenly realized he could not push it up the ramp fully loaded. He and Hemo had worked in tandem to get a full load outside. Restricting himself to smaller loads would reduce the efficiency of the operation, but there was nothing he could do about it. Yet as he worked, his brain was not challenged to do much so he considered whether there might be some way to make the operation work better. Maybe he could make a longer ramp so it was not as steep and he could get a larger load up it. Or he might get a four-wheeled cart somewhere and set up a hoist to draw it up the ramp. A good rig could work a heavy load easily, but setting it up would probably take longer than the time it would save. The thought made him yearn further for such tools as a small cart and a hand-operated hoist. Then he remembered some trucks had a hoist on the front. It was sometimes used to pull the truck out of a snow drift. That would be versatile so he wished for that instead.

With the pick and shovel, he cut a trench in the untouched soil two feet wide and deep as the final soil level extending just past the edge of the house at the midpoint of the front. Using the posthole digger, he went down an additional two feet for the first footer. With one hole finished, he could see even better the scope of the task before him. He began to cut a notch in the soil at the midpoint at the back and heard a very unfriendly klunk before he had filled the wheelbarrow the first time. To this point, he and Hemo had not hit a rock larger than a few inches across. Every rock had been rounded by some remote history in the river. No rock yet was large enough to seriously inhibit progress on lowering the floor. This klunk immediately brought a dangerous image to mind: bedrock. Charles pushed his shovel into the dirt a foot to the side of the klunk and heard a scrapping sound of the shovel on a hard surface. He tried again a foot more to the side and hit only dirt. He lifted a shovelful into the wheelbarrow. He dug in the soft dirt in front of the rock and then flipped his shovel backwards to cut the soil away from the rockface. He drove it down and glanced off the obstruction. The sound he made was not right. He poked at the rock with the shovel and felt a flat surface. He knelt in the dirt and scraped at the object. It was metal, a sheet of metal. He levered his shovel under the edge and worked the object out of the soil. It was a long, low box of a size too small for real pirate booty but right for a child's imitation of a treasure chest. It was made of a heavy gauge steel and even had a padlock on it. Charles thought for a moment it might be good for securing some tools but soon adjusted his thought-- he did not need an old rusty chest to store anything. He went back to the van for something to remove the lock. He did not have a bolt cutter and he expected a hacksaw would not work on the lock since any decent lock would have a hardened shaft. He grabbed a few things and took them back to the box.

Before he went to work, he thought the box just might have some historical significance. It might predate the house, although it appeared modern. He dragged it up the ramp so he could inspect it in the light. It was very ordinary in appearance, heavy, but not much heavier than the empty metal box might have weighed. It did not rattle when he tilted it. It might have once had something painted on it, like a logo. He wondered if it might originally have held a large powertool, like a drill, but that was just his point of view showing through. He tried cutting through the hasp with the hacksaw. It took only a few strokes to see that the blade was not hard enough. He tried to tear the hasp off the box by prying it with a screwdriver, but could not get enough leverage to break it loose. He placed the blade of his small crowbar into the gap behind the lock and hit the other end with a hammer to squeeze it into a position where he could get better leverage, but it would not fit. A drop of sweat fell from his brow onto the top of the box, making a dark spot surrounded by a few tiny dots from the splashing drip. Charles dragged the box over to the shade and laid the tools beside it. He sat back and visualized how they might be applied to the task. "This is fun," he admitted, referring to the contest and the open-ended potential for reward. He fitted the handle of his heavy pliers between the lock and the hasp, and hooked the claw of his crowbar onto the pliers. This arrangement applied a heavy torque on the hasp. He saw it bend slightly. That would be enough; the test was won. A small bend was an opportunity to fatigue the metal, and he worked the hasp back and forth a millimeter each direction until it started to move more easily. The pliers slipped in deeper; the bend got larger. Suddenly, the hasp snapped. He used the big pliers in a more conventional position to bend the hasp further until he got the lock off. The hinge worked smoothly as he lifted the top. All he saw was a heavy layer of plastic wrap over the entire contents. He could not fit his fingers around the edge inside and he was afraid to cut the plastic in case it was covering something dangerous, like rat poison.

When he tried to pry out the contents, his screwdriver bit into the edge of the top layer, and Charles worried he might had damaged something. With the screwdriver, he lifted a piece of plywood out of the box, tearing the now brittle plastic as it came up. A musty smell wafted into his nostrils. He cut away the plastic enough to pull the plywood away. What remained looked exactly like a box of money collected into bundles wrapped by corroded rubber bands.

He felt his senses heighten at the sight. The smell might have been there already, but suddenly became clear. He sat back and listened to his environment. There were some sparrows flitting in the bushes nearby, the dull rush of the river, a faint whoosh of leaves in the tree tops. The sparrows seemed like evidence that no one was lurking in the woods to see what was in the chest. Nonetheless, he flipped the lid back shut and stood up. He kicked the box a little and went back into the basement. He dug a wheelbarrowful of the soil near the ramp, keeping one eye on the chest. He pushed the wheelbarrow up and dumped it near the chest. He loaded the chest into the wheelbarrow and took it back down the ramp. He was not sure why he had tried to hide moving the box. Anyone looking on would have seen it when he dragged it outside.

In the privacy of the cool dark, dirty, and damp room, he took out one of the bundles. The rubber band broke and fell away as soon as he lifted the bundle. It appeared to consist of 100 well-worn twenty-dollar bills, fifty facing one way and fifty facing the other. He rummaged through the chest some more. Most of the bundles were twenties; a few were tens and a few were hundreds.

He collected some samples and two full bundles to be inspected later in better light. Then he cut a tunnel into the side of the dirt wall and reburied the chest. The dirt on top of the new hiding place was undisturbed. He studied the location so he could find it again. Then he took up a few more wheelbarrow loads of soil. He did not really have a plan, but he wanted to think through the implications of his find before anyone knew of it.

To test whether anyone came while he was away, he tied a thread across the ramp and another across the stairway from the first floor. He wiped the bottom of the ramp clear of tracks but tromped heavily when he walked out into the fading daylight. He listened for the sparrows. They were gone. He saw a jay quietly flitting among the branches and imagined that bird would have screamed a warning if anyone were nearby. He gathered his tools, packed them slowly and properly, and drove away. He had put on a show for an audience that certainly did not exist, and the act had occupied his mind away from thinking he had the incredible windfall of a lifetime, many lifetimes.

He did not look at the sample bills when he first got back to his apartment, but went straight into a most comfortable, cool shower. He fought to control his thoughts; there were so many questions. As a question formed, he started to frame it clearly and another interrupted his thoughts; so he pursued that for a moment until a more important one inserted itself. He stopped himself; this confusion was not him. He instructed himself to pick one issue and work it. What first? Oh, to not dwell on the selection too much; pick something. He decided to focus on the possibility the bills were not real. If they were not, most of the other questions would be irrelevant.

He put on fresh clothes with a thought to going out to Smiley's Diner shortly to get away from the treasure, but first indulged his curiosity about the quality of the money. He marked the found bills with a penciled "x" to be sure he did not lose track of which ones they were. Then he took out the strong magnifying glass he sometimes used to look at insects and compared the bills to the ones in his wallet. In the next thirty minutes he learned more about the patterns on currency than he ever expected to care to know. Everything looked good to him, but he could not shake the fear that the bills were counterfeit. He found nothing suspicious in the bundles he had brought home, the date and serial numbers were out of order and the bills were neither especially old or new. He thought there might be a musty odor on the bills but it might have been his imagination. He thought of ironing them to see if it enhanced or removed the smell. This thought reminded him to iron a shirt and get out of the house. It would be good, he imagined, to be seen this evening acting very normally. No one could speculate that he was at home tossing bills into the air in jubilation.

At the diner, as usual, his eyes went first to the cashier's chair. She was not there. He had seen her in the evening sometimes, but, obviously, not this evening.

"Charles!" someone called. He looked the direction of the voice.

"Yo Francis," he called back and smiled at the sight of his friend and the sight of the others in the booth, and strode toward them.

"It's Charles! Have a night out, man," called a voice in another direction.

"Marty!" Charles said to the new voice. He turned his head back and forth a couple times between the booths. "Let me see which booth has better women. Uhhh, I'm going to say it's this one," and he pointed to the booth with Marty. "I'll be right there as soon as I brush off these guys." There were no women at Francis' tabld. He talked to Francis and the others in that booth for a minute and then signaled the conversation was over by putting his hand on Francis' shoulder and waited for him to finish his sentence. "You guys are about finished with dinner. I'll see if there's room with the table equipped with women."

"Don't steal all of 'em!"

On his way to the second table he saw Elizabeth pick up a tray of food from the window to the kitchen. She smiled when she saw him looking at her.

"You're a waitress now?"

"I do it sometimes. It's not a promotion."

"It's better to move around, don't you think? I'd rather walk around than sit in the same place the whole shift. Of course I don't really know what it is like to have your job. And everyone has different tastes..."

"So, do you know everybody here?"

"I lived my whole life here and so did they. So did most people who live here. Not you, of course, but I even know you a little bit."

"Hey Charles! Get you own dinner. That one's mine," someone yelled and a few people laughed lightly.

"I'll see you in a minute," added Charles before he went over to Marty's booth.

"Hi, Charles," all the people at the table said, nearly in unison.

Since Marty had spoken first, he felt like the host and stood up half way to shake Charles' hand. "You remember everybody?" he asked with a wave of his left hand to indicate the others at his table.

"With pleasure," answered Charles as he worked his way around the table visually, looking each person in the eyes and nodding. One was Marty's older sister, whose name Charles could not remember; one was Lesley who had sat behind Charles in English class for the last two years of high school; and the other was Sally, a year ahead of Charles.

"It's all right, Charles. You can sit beside me this time. Nothing will happen to you."

Sally was a tall, sassy woman Charles had known in high school in the general way that he knew everyone in his class. She had always worn her hair short and dressed very stylishly. He knew she was smart but had been more of a social leader than an intellectual, neither category representing the circles in which he had travelled.

"Thank you, Sally. I feel very lucky to have caught all you just as you are starting dinner." Charles answered with bland courtesy but he was intrigued by her teasing invitation. He had always thought she was interesting but had never said anything to her about it and certainly never had any indication that she had noticed him. There were three women with Marty so he did not feel like a fifth wheel.

They talked about Marty's vacation cruise for a few minutes. Charles was not jealous of a Caribbean trip but he did envy two whole weeks without work. Elizabeth came by to take his order for dinner. He wanted to talk to her but it was not a good situation for it, so he satisfied himself with staring into her face while he ordered an open-faced roast beef sandwich with gravy, without having consulted the menu. She hardly looked up from her pad. When she left, Sally asked if his eyes were going to pop out of his head. He just looked at Sally and shoved her gently with his shoulder to make it clear he was not going to follow that line of inquiry.

"Did you get a vacation in yet this year?" he asked her.

"I don't get much time off. I just take a few long weekends. You don't even know where I work do you?"

"No, Sally, I don't. Where do you work?"

"I'm at Franklin Pierce University now."

"Hmm. There're a lot of possibilities there. Frankly, I would like to hear more about what you are doing, but I fear the rest of the table will feel they are eavesdropping on a couple on their first date. May I postpone my questions for a dinner later this week?"

"Charles, are you asking me out?"

"I can hardly recall asking anyone on a date, so I am not sure if that what I was doing, Sally. Before I commit to that concept, I note that in addition to not knowing what you do at Franklin Pierce, I do not know if you are married or if you are actively dating Marty here, but I think it would be pretty lousy if you're going out with Marty for him to take a cruise to Cuba when all you got was a three-day weekend."

"Well, last I knew, you were doing way more than dating Natasha."

"Oh no, Sally. We're not supposed to mention her around Charles," Marty commented and laughed.

"Natasha doesn't mind talkin' about Charles," Lesley added. "I see her all the time. It's a small town, you know."

"I am not that sensitive to mention of my former girlfriend and I know she is not saying angry things. She dumped me, and I even doubt she would mention that. I did no sins against her, but she had good reason to move on. I hope she has found her soulmate. She wants and deserves one."

"Don't you want to know what she says?"

"No, I don't want to talk about Natasha. Talk about her if you want. I promise, if my love life comes up, it will be a very boring topic."

"So when did you break up?" Sally asked.

"Four months, two days, and fourteen hours ago... No, I am not counting like that. She left me last March. To a better point, Marty, are you and Lesley an item? Are you 'dating'?"

"Oooh, Marty's love life is way too complicated for me!" Lesley jumped in.

"Lesley's been my sister's best friend for so long, she feels like another sister. I travel alone these days. It is really very sad," Marty answered. "I'm with you, Charles. No talk about women who aren't with us here tonight."

"That's good," Sally said with ominous intent. "Let's talk about that beautiful waitress. I wonder who she's seeing."

"Who knows? Should I ask her?" asked Marty, looking at Elizabeth.

"I wonder who wishes he was seeing her?" Sally added, looking at Charles.

"If we're going to be young groovy singles, we ought to cover your status. Are you committed to somebody?"

"Just what…"

"No wait, no need to answer. That was IF we were going to be young, groovy singles. That wouldn't be me. I don't do swingin', cool, groovy, fab, rad, or awesome."

"And what do you do?"

"He doesn't do pairs," Lesley interjected, "according to Natasha."

"I love, and can manage most effectively, an open-faced roast beef with gravy."

Before he had a chance to prove this love, he was interrupted by a visit from Francis and the other fellows he had greeted when he first came in, their having now finished their dinners.

"Charles, good to see you, again. You need to get out more."

"I come here a few times a week but I don't recall seeing you around. In fact I had dinner here with Hemo a few nights back."

"Hemo?" exclaimed Francis. "Going out with that lughead is not getting out. Unless you like to get knocked around instead of knocked up."

"Hemo's my pal. He knows how to work and he's working with me some days."

"Oh, I guess he can dig a ditch but don't ask him…"

"Don't go off on my pal, Francis. He's a modest guy but he's a solid thinker. On my jobs, he comes up with ideas on how to do things better. He ought to be in a better job; he can do more."

"Anyway, there's better places to get out than in the diner. I bet you haven't been to Concord since Natasha left."

"Francis, is it?" Sally asked. "We're not talking about Natasha tonight. Not a good topic."

"Oh, yeah, I can see that. All right, Charles. I'll keep looking for you around town. Maybe there's somebody we can agree on. Sally, for instance. Let's talk about her when we meet up."

"I don't know anything about her, Francis. Is she married?"

"Not anymore," Francis said over his shoulder as he left. The three fellows with him smiled and murmured unintelligible syllables of mild courtesy and waved as they went out with him.

"Whoa," Sally said with mock embarrassment and she held the back of her hand across her face like a B-movie actress of the Fifties. Charlie looked at her and thought "What a fine, fine looking woman."

"Charles," She added, "why does everyone say your full name all the time? Do you have some rule about that?"

"Call me 'Charlie'; call me 'Chuck'; just don't call me late for my open-faced roast beef," he intoned dryly and cut a mouthful of the beef and bread to illustrate his point. With that gesture, the conversation moved away from Charles. He ate quickly to catch up with the others since they had begun before him. No one had dessert or coffee. Francis' sister had someplace to go and she rose to leave. Charles rose with her mostly because his mother had taught him that was polite, but he immediately saw it as a good opportunity to leave as well.

"Thank you all for a lovely evening."

"Wait a minute, Charles," Sally held him back. "Did you ask me for a date or were you just lying about wanting to know what I do at Franklin Pierce?"

"Yes, I am interested in hearing about you. It is a bit intimidating to get to know someone in front of observers like this so I have not asked you for a date. Sally *Bradley*, right? If I can overcome my personal demons and pull together enough coins for a night out, I will give you a call. Then we can find out if you will tell me about yourself or just want to tease a poor fellow who was behind you in school. Goodnight Lesley, Marty and Marty's sister. (Sorry, I listened all through dinner to hear your name but no one used it!)"

As he paid his bill he looked at Elizabeth in as friendly a way as he could, but he felt guilty for thinking of Sally who was not his speed, and Natasha whom he might still love, and the found money which was grubby but extremely enticing nonetheless.

Chapter 9 – One Shirtful Is Enough

It was nearly nine o'clock when Charles drove his van onto the space beside his house, listening to his tires grind over the gravel, like a sound from *The Heat of the Night.* He had been thinking of Sally as he drove home, fantasies, really. They were a continuation of the distractions he had used to keep from thinking of the money he found. But now he had some time to devote to that latter topic, to its incredible, implausible, undeniable truth.

He sat in his easy chair, and leaned, as always, away from the arm that was loose, held onto the frame only by the fabric covering. On the nearby crate he used as a table were a pad and paper. He often wrote down ideas as they came to him. Usually he remembered them well enough that the notes were not needed, but the act of writing may have made them more memorable. Without it, they had a way of escaping his mind. He wondered if he could take notes about the treasure without leaving a trail incriminating himself, the notes themselves or the impression they made on the pad beneath. He decided to try thinking through the questions with minimal notes. If he rehearsed reading through them, he might remember everything substantive.

Was the money real or counterfeit? He wrote "reality." How could he be sure? He had already compared it visually to ordinary currency but he was no expert. He could go to a bank in some other city and say that he got one of the bills from a foreigner who seemed anxious to be rid of it and that he wanted it tested. It was probably not needed, but he would like the peace of mind. He would take it to a town in Massachusetts, one large enough to have a solid bank and far away enough that he would not ever be recognized.

Did the money belong to him legally? He thought it did. Testing that question would be hard. He wrote "Legality." Maybe there was a way to ask a lawyer without putting himself in jeopardy. Maybe he could start by asking a lawyer about what was confidential in their consultation. He should at least ask before deciding to break a law that might not exist.

How much was there? That would be easily solved when he dug it up again. He did not need to write anything to remind himself to count it. But that made him think of where to put it, to store it. He wrote "Where."

Would it be taxed? That seemed likely if he revealed it to the government. Generally he liked to be square with the government. In this case, what troubled him was not the government's potential tax; it was whether Robbie would regard the money as his. Charles did not know how confidential his tax records would be. If Robbie suspected the money was in the house and that Charles found it during the renovation, he might find a way to pry into the records. And the record might be in multiple places since Charles would need to consult with someone about how to pay the taxes, if there were any. He could take his chances with Robbie and try to make the money legal or he could keep it all very quiet. Or he could give it to Robbie, but he was not about to take that third alternative. Could he keep it quiet and still use it? He could wait until he sold the house and then use some of it. He could use it slowly, as if his business were doing better than it was. He could only use it for cash transactions since he could not deposit it safely. It would be possible to stretch it over some years so it was never obvious. He could put it on the books as if he had more income and pay taxes on it as it got into his records. He knew of no other way to launder money and did not want to be looking any further into that question.

Charles looked back at his list to see what was missing. He crossed out "Legality." That left him with "reality" and "where." It was a short list of open questions. He considered making a list of ways to spend it but thought it better to wait until he had answered the first two questions. And counted it.

He did not see how going back to the house early the next morning would cause any suspicion if someone saw him do it, but he played with the idea half the night, lying on his back looking only at the backs of his eyelids, and unable to relax, worrying there was some angle he had missed and that it might be better to act casual and normal by staying away for a couple days, except that that was not normal either; he had no set pattern for when he went there.

In the morning, he woke at the usual time. The smart thing to do would have been to get some more sleep, but he thought he would not be able to concentrate at work if he did not move the money to someplace safe. No, that was not his problem. That would have been a reasonable concern and he wanted it to be the source of his antsy feeling but in truth, and he knew it not to be the truth-- he wanted to count it.

He skipped his morning walk in favor of a quick trip to the house. He would still be sure to get to his first job on time so he would look normal to any observer, if there were any observer. During the drive to the house, he began to wonder where to store the money. If someone knew it had been buried, they might come looking for it, although that seemed unlikely since it had been ignored so long. If Robbie knew the money was in the house and Charles needed a way to extricate himself from a dangerous situation, he could claim he had not found it and then he could guide Robbie to the spot and let him find it. In fact, he thought, it might be a good insurance policy to bury some portion of the money in case Robbie came knocking in an insistent way. That did not help him decide on a place to put the money he decided to keep, whether some or all of it.

At the house, he unloaded some tools he was not going to use in addition to his shovel. It made no sense for anyone to be watching him, but it was so easy to make a little extra effort to look logical and feel safer. He went in the front door and banged around in the living room, again for the benefit of anyone watching or listening. But soon he checked the thread he had placed at the top of the stairs and then went down to the basement. He waited for his eyes to adjust and imagined he could see a trench in the dirt bank, reaching right to the place where he had buried his treasure, but there was no trench; no sign at all that anyone had been there. The musty smell of the space and the grit underfoot led to questions about whether it could ever be made into a finished room, a place for a family to eat a fried chicken dinner in front of the television on Sunday night as his family had done. Once his eyes had adjusted to the dark, he went to the ramp he and Hemo had dug and looked for tracks or for any change in the thread he had put out. Everything looked secure.

He had taken thirty minutes to get this far. He needed to leave within fifteen minutes more. It took only one minute to find the chest again; the memory of burying it was as fresh as if he had done it only moments before. He dragged the chest to a convenient place, not near the ramp. To keep the bills clean, he stacked them on the lid of the box as he counted them.

He checked a few bundles and found they were always one denomination and always in groups of a hundred, not a surprising arrangement, but it needed checking. He put one bundle of tens and 25 of the bundles of twenties on one side of his pile so he could take them with him. He tucked them under his shirt and belt. They were bulky enough to require him to let out his belt two holes. He had $51,000 under his shirt. It was a small part of the $850,000 he had counted. He thought about why he was splitting up the hoard and decided he ought to be taking more with him, so he opened up his belt another hole and stuffed ten bundles of hundreds around his waist. Now he had $151,000. If he lost the rest to Robbie, he would still feel successful.

He reburied the chest, just as it had been before. He was running late, but not too badly. He pulled at his shirt to make it loose and then carried his shovel and tools in a way to disguise his bulges, stepped carefully over the thread at the top of the stairs, and walked as casually as he could out to his van.

Chapter 10 - Elizabeth's Real Name

There was a project Charles had promised to complete by Wednesday but he had allowed it to linger and Wednesday had arrived. He thought the situation was tolerable. He worked best with a looming deadline; he noticed how that focused his attention. He did not like his dependence on pressure to become his most productive, but he recognized the characteristic in himself. It was a small project that required gluing some panels into place and waiting for the glue to set before proceeding. He skipped his morning walk and was at the worksite by 6 am. The panels were glued and braced into place by 8:15. He expected the glue needed at least an hour before he could disturb the panels with further work so, to keep himself away, he went out for breakfast.

He thought it would be fun to go to Smiley's and surprise Elizabeth by sitting down for pancakes instead of just taking out coffee and the occasional bagel. And he liked the idea of having pancakes on a weekday without missing any worktime, at least not any worktime against the normal total for a day.

He found a parking space right in front of the diner. He wore no coat for the short walk in brisk air to the door. He stopped with one hand on the door and looked at the trees along the street. He had not fully appreciated the brilliant orange outlining every leaf when driving in. He shook his head in disbelief that life could be so kind to him in so many ways.

Elizabeth looked up from the cash register when he came in. He waved at her, unconsciously wearing a broad smile and then pointed back and forth between to a booth and to himself. She rose and carried a menu to him. "Indemin allesh?" he asked.

"Dehna negn. Indemin alleh?" she answered. Her voice was subdued and she did not look him in the face.

She was already one phrase past his knowledge of Amharic. "I hope you are enjoying this beautiful season! The street outside your window is reaching toward its peak already."

"Yes, it is beautiful," she answered and looked up. There was no enthusiasm in her words. He stared into her face and looked beyond her huge eyes and the beauty that was always there.

"Elizabeth! I think you are not well today."

"I am fine, thank you."

"No Elizabeth, my friend, there is something wrong. You do not need to tell me about it, but you should tell me if there is any way I can help." His money suddenly came to his mind. "You have always been very kind and personable and I would help you if I could, like any friend should." He saw tears fill her eyes. She was not touched by his offer, he knew, but his offer had made her think of her problem.

"Thank you, Charles. I do not think there is anything you can do for me." She hesitated and Charles waited for her to continue. "I have to leave my apartment and I do not know where to go."

"Good, good, Elizabeth. That is something we can fix for sure. You know I have lived here all my life and I know people all over town. I can find a place for you. Please relax about it. When you have some time off, I'll talk to you about what you would like in an apartment."

"No, it is harder than that. We have to leave this town. We have been told to leave but my brother has a job here and we do not know where to go. And he has two children in school and they are very small and it will be very hard for them to start all over in a new place."

"What time do you get off work?"

"Thank you, but it is not a problem for you."

"Let's see about that. We can talk with your brother."

"I get off at eight o'clock tonight."

"Late! I usually see you in the morning. What time did you start today?"

"I started at seven o'clock. I get off from two to five."

"That's still ten hours and a New England siesta."

"Yes, I am saving money for college. I was, but, saving... I don't know; I need this job."

Charles came back at fifteen minutes before eight that evening. He waved to her inside the diner and then waited on the street outside. He thought it would have been a good time to smoke a cigarette if he smoked. She came out soon and took him to a nearby car without saying anything to him. She opened the passenger door, sat down leaving the door open, and said something in Amharic to the man in the driver's seat. Then she said to Charles, "This is my brother, Bekele."

With her face turned to Charles, she closed the car door. The street lamp shone on her in an unfamiliar way, but still revealing her large eyes and distinct eyebrows like a lovely caricature of the woman at the cash register. Her brother got out, walked around the car and shook Charles' hand without quite letting go as he took a step along the sidewalk, pulling Charles along with him. The light on the sidewalk was sufficient to show he was a tall, slender man who walked with a confident air, but Charles could not see his face clearly enough that he could recognize him if they met again.

The brother led their silent walk to a bar less than a block away where they settled in a dark, quiet booth. Despite his calm demeanor, the brother was warmer, less suspicious, than Charles expected. He talked a little about his job at the ball-bearing factory until the waitress took their drink order. He had a whiskey and Charles ordered a local beer. When the drinks arrived, he became quiet, which Charles took as his cue. He considered saying something of himself but realized he had nothing useful to say, nothing to show he was worth trust, so he moved directly to the reason for their meeting. "I understand you are having trouble with your apartment. I know many people in the area and may be able to find someplace to live."

The brother explained that their landlord had told them to leave. This was not a disaster in Charles' view, until he also learned that this conflicted with the lease and that the landlord had given as a reason that their food smelled too un-American, and that the landlord actually represented a conglomerate which controlled all rentals in the area and would prohibit their finding a place anywhere nearby. All this encouraged Charles as being so far from legal that he could surely get them relief. In this time and place, the institutions would be supportive of the immigrants. ...Unless they were illegal themselves.

He asked about citizenship and green cards for all adults in the household and received assurances that the brother understood the regulations and had followed them. Still he asked if he could review the documents one day. Charles did not know what they should look like, but he figured he could look them up on the internet and, since he had money (probably), he could even hire a lawyer.

He looked at the brother's shadowed face, unable to read his expression but consoled by his appreciative voice. The brother ought to be looking into Charles' motives. Charles realized he ought to be looking into those motives too. Was he trying to help this attractive woman so she would feel some substantial obligation to him or just so she would think well of him? Or was he trying to help her because she deserved help he might be able to give? He liked her but could not conceive of coupling with her. He would like her to appreciate him, to know his name and talk to him about things beyond the weather.

If he gave her money or spent money on her, he would have to abandon any personal ambitions with her. It would feel like prostitution, as if he were trading something personal for money. But if she did not know he spent the money, it would not get in the way; it would be a pure act of generosity.

With matters as they were, having been dropped by Natasha for his passive infidelity, failing to earn enough in his business to support a family or grow the business, lusting after Sally whom he scarcely knew, and sneaking to benefit from money he did not earn, he thought a pure act might do his self-image more good than leveraging a good impression from a beauty.

"Bekele, I do not understand your situation perfectly, of course, but what I am hearing from you sounds like something we can fix. We do not need to involve your sister in this very much. It seems you hold the lease and are therefore the central person at issue. Let me talk to some local officials and do some

160

research on the internet. Can I review your lease and
your green card and Elizabeth's green card, say,
sometime tomorrow? Let me think what I am doing
tomorrow— Thursday. Pretty busy. I won't be able to
do much until after five. You know, like you, I have to
work. When do they expect you to be out of your
apartment?"

"He said seven days. And I should be out of
the area, not just move somewhere around here. Who
is Elizabeth?"

"Elizabeth? Yes, sorry. That is the name I
heard for your sister. I know it is not her real name. I
do not really know her."

"She is 'Makeda'."

"Makeda, OK, thank you, ...Makeda. I will
remember that when I go to the diner. I will not take
the papers anywhere, just see them. But after I talk to
someone who knows more about these things than I do
so I know what to see."

"And your name is Charles?"

"Yes, here, I will write out my name and phone
number."

"But you must be careful. This landlord may
destroy our things if he is angry. I think he is a rough
person."

The waitress came near but did not stop at their
table. Nonetheless, Charles did not respond right
away; it showed he was being discrete. "I can see that
the message he has given you is very aggressive. I will

not let anyone know I am looking into your affairs, not until you agree on what we should do next."

Charles could not think of anything else to ask. "Do you want to meet tomorrow night so I can look at the papers?"

"Yes, I can show them to you."

"Let's meet in your car so no one sees us working together. I can see you when you pick up Makeda. Is she off at 8:00 again? Should we meet at 7:30 on the street near Smiley's?"

"I am not sure what time she finishes. We can ask her. But I think that will be a good time."

"I am just a carpenter, really just a handyman. I know only as much about the law as a regular American and I think I know as much about this town as most folks who have lived here all their lives. Maybe not. Sometimes I find I don't know this place very well... Anyway, we can see if there's something to help you. The treatment you are getting seems very wrong."

Bekele stood up. "I can thank you for trying to help. That is all anyone can do."

Bekele insisted on paying for their drinks and then they went to talk to Makeda, still sitting in the car. They did not explain their small plan to her; just asked when she would get off work on Thursday. Charles assumed Bekele would talk to her more about their conversation.

Charles felt like a superhero. He had a secret power. He had a way to use his good fortune, a literal fortune, to someone else's benefit. If he could use it to help the lovely Makeda, he would not worry so much about people learning he had not earned it. It would not hurt that Makeda thought well of him even if he could never hope for an intimate relationship with her. His help might make him her hero, although he would not play it for that purpose. Her life would be too hard to understand and to fit into his. If he could not successfully live with Natasha, who had so much in common with him, he could not live with a woman so completely different from himself.

Tomorrow, he would look for a lawyer, start with clarifying what was confidential and then look into whatever issues of ownership of treasure in a basement, of taxation on such buried treasure, and of money laundering as seemed safe but certainly get some pointers on handling evictions.

Chapter 11 - Sally

Saturday morning came around again and Charles was tempted by the exhaustion in his body to remain in bed late. He searched through his sleepy brain for an alternate time to rise, such as when he had had slept so long that he was not tired, or when the sun was fully up, or when Natasha called him to breakfast with the smell of bacon and coffee and fresh baked bread heavy in the air. This last fantasy was so disturbing he rose quickly, suddenly no longer interested in relaxation. He sometimes talked himself out of his walk on Saturday morning but now he was wide awake and ready to meet his obligations to healthy routine. Still, weekends were not workdays and he was looking forward to operating later in the day at a weekend pace.

It did not take more than two minutes to dress for a walk in late summer so he was out the door very shortly after resolving the debate over whether to get up at all. In his weekend mode, he went over his priorities for the day. The only plan was to work on the house with Hemo. It had been fun and productive on the previous weekend so Charles was now wondering if he might hire Hemo more regularly. Could he keep him busy through the week and would Hemo be productive enough to cover the twenty dollars an hour he deserved? Charles jogged into the curve at the end of his street, feeling wide awake with the cool dawn air filling his lungs. He forced himself to hold back, saving energy to keep running the rest of the way. He focused on making his footsteps as silent as possible on the pavement. When he thought he had the motion of his run adjusted to be as smooth and quiet as possible, he returned to his vision for hiring Hemo. And then he shook his head at his own stupidity. He needed to be focusing on the unanswered question of where to hide the money. His superpower could turn against him if he were not smart about the details. He suggested options for hiding the cash and every one came up obviously wrong. Leaving it with someone would bring in complications he could not control. He knew no one reliable enough to hide it without knowing what it was and did not want to involve anyone by revealing the nature of his cache. "Natasha might be good for it. She would be reliable. People would not suspect her... What a stupid idea that was. Of course people might suspect her involvement. Not everyone could know how completely they had separated." But thinking while running was never productive, so he was not discouraged. There was time to develop a safe vault. His immediate plan was to keep it in the back of his mind all day and to have a solution jump out at him while he was in the shower after work. It would be too much of a coincidence for anything critical to happen on the last day before he took care of it. He did not believe in coincidences, just in the inexorable playing out of the odds.

On his way back he picked up the pace of his steps as he rounded the turn onto his street. He would bring it home strong and stretch out on the front stoop until he caught his breath and cooled down enough for a shower. He was glad he had gotten up on time. He could stop off at the diner for breakfast before meeting Hemo.

He pulled up suddenly before reaching his house. Someone was standing on his stoop, peering through the front window. He ducked immediately, hiding behind a parked gray pick-up truck. He noticed his breath coming heavily and felt his heart pound. It was just from running hard, he told himself. They would be looking for money again. Did they know he had it? Did they know for sure it had been in the riverside house somewhere? He had hidden the part he took home under the insulation in the attic, between the third and fourth joist on the end farthest from the trap door. It would be hard to find and they had not looked very hard last time. No hiding place was perfect. He looked up the street to see if an old green pick-up was in the neighborhood.

Charles snuck around the edge of the gray pick-up to see if anyone else was around. It was barely dawn, somewhere near six am. Nothing good could come of a visit at this hour but there was no way to ignore it. He leaned around the truck to get a good view of the intruder. It was a tall, slender woman wearing shorts and wearing them very well. He found himself appreciating her shape. Sadly for him, it was not Natasha. He stood up and called out, "Hey! Anybody in there?"

"They said I needed to get here by dawn to catch you, but I didn't think they were serious about it." It was Sally and she seemed irritated.

"Sorry Sally. If I had any hope of your being here this morning, I would have stayed in and brewed some coffee."

"You never called me."

"Yes. I am an awkward fellow, lacking confidence in relation to the most desired woman in town. I figured you were tipsy or showing off to your friends the other night."

"You said you were interested."

"It was a sort of academic interest, not a practical one. You know, that little talk at Smiley's is the first time we ever spoke to each other?"

"Yeah, I know," she posed coyly. Charles could see that she was used to having her way with thoroughly ordinary young men like himself. He looked into her face. The light was not strong in the long shadow of the house, but he did like what he saw. It did not make sense, he knew, to desire her just on the basis of her regular features and tight skin. At least her aggressive demeanor was something he could admire in her personality. She let him stare into her, letting her physical appeal have its effect on his will.

"I'm not dressed for entertaining, but you can come in while I cool down. I am intensely curious as to why you would trouble yourself to come here."

Charles turned the knob on the unlocked door and gestured for her to enter. As he stepped inside he turned on the light.

"Oh god," Sally exclaimed, "this looks like college student housing."

"It's a good deal better than I had for my brief college career, but I take your point."

"I would have thought Natasha would have fixed it up better than this."

"Natasha deserved better. I can't say she demanded it. The shabby state of my place did not send her away."

"Maybe we don't need to talk about her."

She perched on the edge of the couch. Her knees touched the crate Charles had covered with scraps of hardwood flooring. The shape of her legs was well defined in this posture, pleasantly to Charles, while her torso was loosely covered in a bright cotton print, also pleasantly so in Charles' opinion.

"You see, one of the advantages of this poor place is that it's small enough I can hear whatever you say in the living room no matter where I am. May I offer you an orange juice? I could make a pot of tea or some drip coffee." Charles went into the kitchen area without leaving her line of sight. He did not want to sit in front of her while he was sweaty. It might have made all the furniture seem unclean.

"Can you make a cup of coffee?"

"I'm a handyman. Not only that, I have good taste, even if my home does not display it. I can make toast too. Want some? I have two kinds of jam and I don't mean jelly."

"Are you totally broke or are you saving for a round-the world trip? I thought you were one of the smart guys in school."

"Oh, c'mon. You never thought about me in any respect!"

"You weren't in my circle. I hung out with Rich and those jock friends of his. They liked you. They thought you could be a jock but you had other things you wanted to do more."

"They were wrong. Back then there was nothing I would rather have done than star in those major sports and hang out with the likes of you." Charles washed his hands as conspicuously as possible and dried his hands while facing her.

"But you were smart, right? Went to college and all?"

"I went. Didn't finish. Can't say it was all that hard, especially the little place where I went, but it proved I wasn't too smart. I let the chance to do it go by, I guess." Charles started the coffee.

"Doesn't mean you're not smart. Everyone says you can do anything."

"Maybe you're talkin' to someone who's not so smart. I'm a handyman and I can make stuff, mostly stuff that people make rather than corporations. Not cars, I don't do cars. But houses and furniture and clocks. Mostly I fix stuff, but that is passé now. The economy is not interesting in fixing things. I like rebuilding and repairing. There is an ethical pleasure in it for me. We replace too much too often. It is ultimately an inefficient use of our resources. I feel the earth being used up."

"Is this house a sample of your reliance on rebuilding?"

"This isn't my house; I just live here. I rent. I own a house. It is an example of my rebuilding, or it will be when it is finished. That's where my resources are; there and in my business: tools and such."

"You have a house somewhere you are rebuilding? You mean 'flipping'?"

"Yes, you could call it that. I don't call it that. Hey, I bet I can get a shower before the coffee is done. Do you mind if I try?"

"Knock yourself out."

Sally leaned back in the couch when Charles went into the bedroom to collect his clothes for the day. She looked around. The living room bore the look of a household just one full step above American poverty except for a few out-of-place items. Maybe he did have taste, mostly hidden but waiting for the money and time to reveal itself. Maybe his comment on taste was a weak attempt at saying he liked her. She got up and went into the kitchenette. She looked in the cabinets. They were extremely neat. Everything was clean, but there were no appliances or wares of quality. She listened to the gurgles and watched the drips of the coffee maker. Its pace increased for a few moments and then began to dissipate. The gurgles ceased and the drips came slower. She looked for coffee cups or mugs.

"Cabinet by the window."

"Damn, you scared me. You that fast at everything?" Sally turned to see him leaving the bathroom, dressed but for his shoes, hair unkempt, as the drying towel had left it.

"I assume you realize, and may even be asking if I realize, that not everything should be done fast. On the whole, my business would be doing much better if I were faster at things. I tend to do something different every day and never get really good at it. I mean, at work."

"And what is it you do well away from work?"

"Probably not for me to say. But everyone should know what he does well. Take some pride in something, you know." Charles marveled at her legs while trying not to reveal that he was looking at them. Her calves hung from the bone, leaving a soft dip running along the side of each leg, the muscles carried their shape independent of the bone. She was lean and tight. It bothered him that he would care about something so biological, just as he was bothered that he remained constantly aware that her facial bones formed a perfect feminine image, independent of the person inside. Why should these extremely minor details of her construction matter as they did?   He even wondered if he so admired them because they reflected the most admired girl he knew when he was forming his taste in femininity.

"I was good at being a teenager."

"You damn sure were."

"And you didn't like school, and you know you're nobody's fool.'"

"That why you're here today! You think I was not a fool? I like to think that too, but I can't. And these years later, I am trying to be part of the machine in my own way." He emphasized the last phrase: in my own way. It was a boast, but it was true too.

"You know your Pink Floyd... I was in the machine. I was the fucking machine back then. I thought it would last, like all teenagers think. It's OK that I grew up. Maybe I had to grow up since everyone else was doing it. Even in college, it was different. Everyone didn't know everyone else. I felt I was on display, not me, just the part of me people could see. I didn't attract the best kind of guys.   I knew there were good guys out there but I was like everybody else, picking my mate on the basis of what I could see. There are good guys, aren't there. Aren't you one? Natasha says you are."

"Too fast. You talked to Natasha about me? Why do I have the feeling I am trying out for something here. And it is something for which I am entirely unqualified although I sure wish I could hope to someday be with you. No, I can't even wish for that. It is too demanding. I cannot even imagine it. You were never the creature of my fantasies. You have always been too implausible. But put these discomforts aside for the moment while I answer your question since I have a rock solid answer for you. Am I a good guy? Most days I would say yes since I am an extremely normal guy and I think man is good. That is my default position. But this is not an ordinary day for me. It is not an ordinary week and it became something else even before the implausible Sally turned up at dawn. It is not ordinary because I honestly and sincerely am planning to become a superhero, and it feels great. That would make me good compared to the typical man."

"Oh no, you don't do comics do you?"

"Not at all. And I don't do fantasy either; else I would be trying to take you more seriously. No, I am planning to do a very, very good thing, something few people could do and no one but me would do."

"And what is that?" A tone of disappointment was in Sally's voice. She revealed it willingly, tired of men's boasts.

"Ah, there's the rub. It is secret and shall always be so. That's part of why it feels like being a superhero. But a couple of beneficiaries will know it was me so the situation does not allow for the purest charity."

"Not good. Why should I believe you?"

"It does not matter if you believe, except that I like everyone to believe me all the time. I like being known as a forthright man. Why should I lie to you? I have no hope of attaining you. And if you imagined I was worth looking into, because you did not really know me or because Natasha was generous in her comments, our meeting this morning will confirm I am not in the right league."

"You still in love with Natasha?"

"She might ask if I ever was. The word is too heavy. We hardly ever agree on what it means. I have no more hope of getting back with her than I do of getting with you. She knows me well enough to know I'm not what she wants and I know her well enough to know I'm not what she wants."

"I just want to know a good guy."

"I know a few.   Like I said, I think men are normally good. They, we, most of us, want what we earned. We wish no ill on others, not after we have put aside the childishness of taking games to be reality. Most of us understand it is necessary to earn something. We know it feels better to have it when it's earned. I don't mean just money here. Does that make most of us good? Good enough for me but not,

I should think, for the fantasy Sally inexplicably sitting in my ragged living room."

"Earning? That's what you think make a man good?"

"Largely that. And doing little harm to the planet."

'So your superhero act will be earning something?"

"No. It's not about that at all. My philosophy is not that elegant. But no hints. A secret is secret."

"Will you tell me a secret? Not that one. Not one about Natasha. Another one."

"Sally, it is no secret that you are an exciting woman. It's not just what I see, and I could tell you what it is but it would sound as if I had hope and I do not. Let me go to work. I work on my house on Saturdays."

"I know when I am being kicked out. You were nice to me today. Honest, I think. You should have more hope." Sally stood up and handed her coffee mug to Charles. He looked into her face when she was near and she leaned forward and kissed him on the cheek. He hesitated for the merest instant, then turned his head to kiss her cheek but she was already moving away. He nearly reached out and held her, to show her he could give a small buss too, but it would have been even more awkward than missing her cheek the first time. He put the mug in the kitchen sink beside his own and ran a little water to fill them so the coffee would not set a stain. He heard the door close behind Sally. There was no time for Smiley's this morning. It might be better that he did not turn up in front of Elizabeth at every chance; he might seem to be measuring his advantage over her.

Chapter 12 – Amin Leaves Home

A typical boy is confused in his fourteenth year by his changing body. His hands and feet are not where they were the year before and, sometimes, not where they were the day before, making it very hard to move gracefully. No matter what he has heard about this growth which he longs to achieve, it is not what he expects. And the changes in glandular secretions bring even more curious effects in voice timbre, skin eruptions, and innate desires. The changing environment for boys of this age and their relationship to the environment is further confusing. New expectations arise from others about their behaviors and their responsibilities. They do not understand why their parents are still attractive or are suddenly unattractive, why they and other authorities do not understand what is most relevant anymore, or why...

There is good in it for most boys. They like being as tall as their mothers and they like collecting and sharing fantasies, boasts and lies within groups of their peers, gangs, that can intimidate boys outside the group, as they were a year or two earlier. And these groups let them play out their revised desires for sex, or their lack of such desires, without having to meet any actual targets of potential sexual desire.

Amin was less confused at fourteen than most. He was less concerned than most about the changes in himself.   He watched them with small interest and without truly comprehending that they were the process defining what he would be as an adult. His desires changed more slowly than his body. His toys changed but he still had toys. He stopped strategic battles played out with his collection of small sticks in lieu of plastic soldiers but he preferred to play the made-up ball games with his sister rather than the organized, competitive games the older boys played after school. He was taller than average for his class and sprouted dark hairs above his lip, enough that his mother and father had a small argument one day about which of them would teach him to shave. His mother won, though she would not do the task. His father was irritated that she had been so insistent he accepted the duty and immediately stormed into the room where Amin was doing his homework. He nearly grabbed Amin by the back of his shirt and dragged him into the bathroom, but it was such a stupid thing to do to an innocent child or boy or young man, he hesitated. And then he thought about what to say to his son and a few good ideas came to mind, not about what to say or how to say it, but about how this could be a time to build his relationship with his maturing son, to treat him in a new way, not merely instructing him, but offering guidance. "Amin!" he called firmly but not in an unfriendly way. "Yes, Daddy?" Amin answered, using a diminutive that proved he was still a child in his way. Amin's father saw he was sweet and innocent as a child and wished it were possible to stay that way. He remembered wanting to grow up fast himself and saw no such interest in Amin. Was it wrong to remain a boy a little longer? It was not possible to delay it much further, his body was about to take over. Amin's father decided to show Amin how to shave and not to say it was necessary to do it. It should be enough that the lesson had been given, enough to communicate that the act should be done, but it was better to let Amin choose to do it.

Amin took his lesson in silent embarrassment. Such personal things were not normally shared with his parents, not in recent years, and if they had to be endured, it would have been more normal to do them with his mother. And yet there was a certain logic to receiving this lesson from his father and there was nothing disgusting in it to explain his embarrassment. Amin was surprised when his father shook his hand and left him standing alone in the bathroom. He had been allowed to choose whether to shave when he was hardly ever allowed to choose anything. He was inclined to do it another day soon. That would demonstrate it was his own choice, a point he suddenly felt important. It would be good to carry around the knowledge of how to shave while people looked at his faint mustache and thought he did not possess that knowledge. He curled his lip over his upper teeth and looked in the mirror. His hairs stood out, long, thin, and sparse. He looked more advanced than his peers, but not better than them. He visualized shaving.

There was not much to know about it. The lesson from his father was mostly a matter of giving him confidence and permission. He inspected his cheeks. There was a downy layer that did not need to be cut away although his father had said it could be shaven too. It was obvious his father wanted him to shave. And that his father thought it was for his own good somehow. So he shaved. It took only a minute. The next time he shaved, he would have more hairs but he would spend less time removing them. The hair grew back, of course, yet it was nearly two months before he shaved again.

The day after his first shave, Amin learned why his parents had pressed the issue. The family was about to leave on a grand vacation, going farther than Amin ever thought he would be from Agadir (which is in Morocco), to meet relatives he had never thought he would meet, famous relatives, by his accounting, the branch of the family that had been to Mecca and had settled across the sea and become rich. His parents had not told him or his younger sister of the trip before the morning they departed. Maybe they saw no reason to consult with children. Amin spent the morning absorbing the exciting news and packing what he would take. Packing did not take up much time as his parents allowed him only one small sack to carry his belongings. He brought a change of underwear, a change of socks, an extra shirt, a jacket to wear in the evening when the dry desert air becomes cold quickly, and the razor his father gave him. His sack was not full. His sister's sack was twice as full as his so he carried them both.

They left after the Dhuhr prayers, that is, around 1:00 in the afternoon. They rode on a flat platform pulled by a tractor to Essaouira, arriving early enough for the Maghrib prayers. They slept that night in the house of a friend and left the next day on a coastal ferry that took two days to reach Rabat. That night they stayed on the docks, which were full of travelers like themselves, a friendly place with plenty of enticing food in varieties and odors new to Amin and his sister. His parents authoritatively drifted among the street vendors and selected small samples of things the children should try. It was hard for Amin to believe even more exotic experiences lay ahead.

In the morning they climbed aboard a steamship. Those days on the small, open ferry to Rabat were now only a minor stage in the grand plan, but they waited all day without moving from the docks. On board the ship, there was little to see in the spaces they were allowed to roam, but Amin could scarcely rest with the thrill of exploration running though his body, fed by stories his father told of the historical places they would pass. Finally, early in the second day, the ship passed through the Pillars of Hercules and began its passage across the Mediterranean to Beirut. Amin was surprised not to see the southern Pillar, the one on the African side of the Strait of Gibraltar, but men have wondered where it is for millennia.

They saw no coastline for the next three days, which did not surprise Amin, given the vast sea they were crossing. He was not even disappointed by the unchanging view from the porthole since he was not allowed to sit on the deck to watch the scenery anyway. He was soon to be surprised to find no cedars covering the hillsides of Lebanon, another absence no one explained to him.

It took all day to find the relatives they were to meet. Amin was sure they had passed them on the docks more than once during the day, but that his parents had not recognized them. They were very warm in their greetings, but not very familiar. Everyone seemed pleased by the fact of the visit, independent of the individuals involved. And that should have been fine; the trip should have been an opportunity to grow, to know new people, and to benefit from their knowledge of the world.

Amin was not clear about how these people were related to him or what he should be learning from them. He saw the trip as being to a different place, rather than to different people. He was also unsure about the geography of the next part of their trip. His parents did not bother to tell him what they had planned. He knew they were supposed to be going to Jordan but he was never sure if they actually crossed the international border before the rocket landed on their party.

He did not know anything at all for a few days. There was a moment when they were riding in a very crowded car, his sister sitting in his lap, both of them listening to the men in front, and then it was much later and he was lying beside the wreckage. The air was full of smoke and noise and movement. He sat up. No one was paying any attention to him, but someone had taken him out of the car. He looked back at the tangled metal, unsure he was seeing the car although he could see painted scraps in the shade the car had been. He was bleeding himself from some shrapnel wounds, but did not feel incapable of walking away.

Two months later, when he was out of the hospital and living in a refugee camp, he was told he was lucky, lucky to have survived and lucky to have relatives in the United States who would buy his ticket to go live with them.

Chapter 13 - A Joint Resolution

It was Amin's idea to hike up Mt. Adams. He knew Charles and Hemo worked together on Saturdays so he proposed it for Sunday. It was the first week in October. Amin, like everyone else in New England, knew the foliage was peaking in the White Mountains but that was not why he wanted to go out with his friends. He could not say what was missing, but his life had developed a dull routine. He was not bold enough to make a change, but he was bright enough to see the need for it. His routine did not trouble him for the first years when it developed after school because he did not realize how stable it might be. Nothing had been stable in his life for so many years before then, he was pleased to know the next day would be like the past day.

It was Hemo's talking about doing better that started Amin's dissatisfaction. Amin saw it as a privilege to look for improvement in his lot and he struggled with whether he could have that privilege. He could believe that he deserved anything Hemo deserved, and Hemo took this privilege for granted even if he had been unable to get beyond the stage of aspirations. But when Hemo started working regularly for Charles and doing it at a higher salary, Amin felt the envy creep under his skin so he itched at night while trying to sleep and sometimes during the day when his routine gave him time to think. At the men's shop where he worked, he heard people his age talking among themselves with boundless enthusiasm about hiking in the wilderness. They said Mt. Adams was the best hike in New Hampshire, although their idea of what is best seemed to have included a large degree of difficulty. It was not a way to advance in work or to find a wife, but it would get him out of his rut for a day at least and maybe give him better things to think about afterwards too. It was slightly possible he would like it enough that he would become a hiker with his own enthusiasms and would plan his own excursions with a circle of young, healthy, energetic, and uncomplicated people. He called Charles; Charles would know how to arrange it.

"Hello."

"Hello Charles. It's Amin."

"And it is a fine thing to be, too! Good to hear from you! What have you done since I saw you last?"

"What have I done? That is just it. I haven't done anything."

"I don't believe it. You have more dates than an oasis in Morocco. Do you know how many that is, Amin?"

"I don't remember Morocco. I was thinking we might go on a hike in the wilderness. Have you ever been up Mt. Adams?"

"Mt. Adams? I would not call that wilderness. We don't have wilderness in New England anymore. But whatever you call it, Mt. Adams would be an ambitious trip. It would be a right fine trip too. You were thinking of going overnight?"

"Overnight? No, just for a day. Sunday. Unless you can take off on Saturday too."

"...Could. I could take off Saturday. I need someone like you to help me get away from work. It's too easy to just keep at it. Have you ever backpacked? It'd be a tough haul. I don't mean we would go out to set any records, but it's a rugged walk any way you do it."

"You tell me. Can I do it?"

"Of course you *can*, Amin. I'm not so sure you would enjoy it. Maybe we could do a day trip up a mountain and you could see how much you like tired legs, aching back, and sore shoulders. I love those things, myself."

Amin liked the sound of the struggle. It was just what he imagined he needed. But he thought it would sound vain to say so, even though it did not sound vain when Charles said it. Charles was not just imagining he liked the rough road; he lived it, or so Amin thought.

"If we just go for the day, we could have some others along. I mean, I'd like the chance to talk with you but it's nice to have more. Maybe Hemo would go."

"I *know* Hemo would go. I'll ask him."

"And maybe a couple women could come along too. Hemo would like that. I could ask a couple, like someone for Hemo. You could bring Sally.”

“Sally! Where did you ever get that idea? Me and Sally? I wish!”

“I got the idea from her.”

“You’ve been talking to Sally? And talking about me? That makes no sense.”

“I wasn’t really talking to her about you. She’s friends with Nikki. You know I am going out with her a lot these days. You know her?”

“I don’t think so.”

“Yeah, why would you? She’s OK. Good lookin’, I guess. Nice too. But not really good for me. She’s too regular. I don’t know what she wants. I don’t even know what’s different about her. She’s like just a really regular, but good looking, woman. Maybe too young. She only a year younger than us, but she hasn’t done anything.”

“You, me, and Hemo; reluctant bachelors.”

“What about Sally?”

“No way. No Sally. I don’t know how my name even came up. You know she’s too hot for me.”

“No she’s not!”

“Oh yes she is and you know it and she knows it. I did talk to her one day a while back and she was talking like she might be looking for a new boyfriend but I was a very weak candidate for her.”

"She's probably looking for a new husband. You know she got divorced after just a few months of being married."

"No, we didn't get into that. She saw my poverty. I won't be on her husband list."

"She was talking about you and it sounded like she was more than interested."

"Maybe she got interested when I didn't fall all over her. That must seem odd in her experience. Anyway, this sounds like high school again. 'Sally likes you!' There is nothing about high school I want to relive. Let's get outside: you, me and Hemo. We'll see if we want to do an overnight. We can go up Mt. Adams partway. We'll save the best route to the top for another day. This will be the perfect weekend to see the trees. We just need to get away from the crowds. It won't be wilderness, but we can fake it. I don't know the routes, but I can ask around. I do know it'll be a long drive to get up to the trailhead. Let's meet here at 5 am on Sunday. Can you do that? Or here's a better idea; get over here on Saturday after dinner. We'll get to sleep early."

"Good, good. It's all good. You'll call Hemo, right? Then I'll see you on Saturday night."

"Saturday, man!"

Charles was dreaming of a good day back in college, a day in his senior year, though he never had a senior year, when he was ready for the exam, anxious to get into the room to take the exam and prove to himself he was ready, knowing he was close to finished with school and would soon be sending letters to the companies where he wanted to start his career. In the dream he was not sure what area his career would address; he was not concerned about what the work was, only that he do it well. And then something began to go wrong: the sky darkened and the other students crowded near, bumping him accidentally, disturbing him, disrespecting him. Someone was tapping on his book. Charles stood up, and pushed the person away, ready to give or take a beating. The person stood away from Charles, surprised at Charles' aggressiveness with so little provocation. And the tapping continued. Charles looked down at his book but no one was touching it. He woke up. There was a tapping, a knocking on the window. Charles thought he would not turn on the light because it might chase away the cause of the sound and he was becoming very curious. He rolled quietly onto the floor in the dark and crept close to the window, looking into it from the side. There was just a faint light from the nearing dawn, enough to tell someone was there. Charles blinked to clear his eyes. He could not see the face, but he suddenly recognized the profile of thick fingers; it was Hemo. He looked to the clock. Hemo has arrived a couple minutes before the alarm would go off. Charles appreciated the odd arousal. He hated to force himself to get out of bed on mornings that began earlier than usual. He tapped on the window and then went to the open the front door.

He turned the light on as he entered the living room. Amin was sleeping on the air mattress Charles had loaned him. It was a test to see how much Amin minded sleeping on it. He could have shifted to the couch during the night; Charles had not suggested it was a test but here he was sleeping soundly even with the light on. Charles pulled the front door open; Hemo came a moment later, muttering loudly, trying to sound like a drill sergeant. "Rise and shine, you maggots!"

Charles held a finger to his own lips, "Shhh, Amin is still in the arms of Morpheus."

Hemo hesitated for a moment before getting Charles' point although he was not sure what Charles had said. "Well, we can fix that right away!" He looked at Amin and then went to the sink and ran some water into a glass. Charles watched as he stood over Amin and let a drop fall onto his face. Amin opened his eyes quickly but did not jump much.

"What was that?" he asked but he was not sure what he was talking about or who was standing over him.

"Into every life some rain must fall," quoted Charles with dramatic intonation.

"Are you quoting Shakespeare at this hour of the day" asked Hemo.

"I don't think so. I got it from the Ink Spots."

"Hemo?" Amin wiped off his face. "Damn, what time is it? Am I late?"

"No. Are you thirsty? Open wide."

Amin sat up suddenly and held his arm in front of his face to protect himself although the threat was too small to merit the force of a forearm. Hemo made a quick move with his empty hand, as if it could toss water on Amin. Amin flinched a little, still not awake enough to know what Hemo was doing.

"I offered to pick up Hemo on the way out but he said he would make us toast and coffee." Charles said while watching the little skit his two friends were performing. "So Hemo, you better get on with it. We got well organized last night and will be ready for that continental breakfast in five minutes. You know where everything is, right?"

"I can manage. I'm not just a pretty face, you know."

"Make mine a double. I'm driving.'

Before they had gone ten miles from the house, Charles was the only one awake. He felt alone in the van, watching the dawn brighten into day while speeding toward a mountain trail. He only wished his knapsack were packed for a few days. As it was, he could sense the day passing while he was enclosed in his moving metal box. And yet he was pleased with the view. The small towns, each with a library, white church steeple, and town hall facing a commons were waking to their small existences. The traffic was light, of course. Charles and his van knew the roads and were at home. In all this familiarity, the scene was not ordinary. Autumn was showing itself. As they went north, it was more and more conspicuous. He kept in mind the reddest tree he passed and the brightest orange until he passed another that might have been even brighter. When the sun came up and shone through the leaves from behind, the trees could look gaudily artificial except that they were actually completely wild, edges of woodlands, not gardens. He smiled at each new garish variation on the theme. Driving gave him the chance to move from scene to scene with never a chance to absorb all that any scene offered. He was stunned by the richness of life; he longed to stop the van, to rouse his friends and stand amid the bizarre colors, breathe in the odors and dust of their decay, and be part of the season.

After an hour, Amin moved for the first time. "If Hemo's going to sleep, I should sit next to the window."

"Shotgun, we call it."

"How come?"

"In the days of stage coaches in the American west, the myth says a guy with a shotgun sat beside the window to defend the coach. If you want to sit there, all you have to do is be the first to call 'shotgun'."

"I didn't heard Hemo say 'shotgun'."

"No, I didn't either."

A few moments passed before Amin said gently, "Shotgun."

Charles pulled the van to the side of the road next to a pond. The pond was close to the road but the water level was several feet lower. Trees closely overhung the water so much that no blue showed to their vision. The surface was a mix of reflected and floating leaves, the reflected ones seeming more real since their transmitted light was the only illumination for the dark cavern.

Charles called sharply "Hemo!"

"Wha? Are we there?"

"Hemo, we are never there; we are always here. That just the way it works. Let Amin sit by the window."

"Aw, c'mon. I can't sleep in the middle."

"So don't sleep. You're missing New England at its finest. Besides, he called 'shotgun'."

"Amin! I didn't know you knew that one! Sure, take the window in the best of American tradition."

He stepped out of the van, let Amin out, and then got back in and shut the door before Amin could get in. Charles just continued looking forward while the motor idled. Amin stood outside shaking his head until Hemo opened the door for him. Hemo laughed a little and shifted to the middle of the seat. Before Amin could get back inside the van, however, he heard a rushing sound behind him and he ducked without looking back. There was a flight of warblers arriving in the bushes around the pond. They were not calling, but were noisy from the rustle of their wings. Amin put his hand on the van door but watched the warblers for a moment more, trying to see any one bird clearly. He saw flashes of tawny yellow but never saw the full shape of an individual bird. Neither Charles nor Hemo knew why Amin was staring at the pond, but they granted him this moment to his thoughts. Amin smiled at the movement, and soon accepted the general twittering was sufficient for this experience.

"Reach in the back before you settle in, Amin, and grab a few apples out of that bag. They're from Barnard's orchard. Just the kind I love, snapping hard and tart."

Hemo drew out his sheath knife and cut off slices of apple. Amin bit noisily into his. Charles held the apple in his right hand and drove with his left, reserving his strong hand, the right, for the more important task. No one commented further on their quality but the temporary devotion to them revealed their shared opinion. Charles was first to finish. He lowered his window and tossed out the stub. Amin sucked on the core awhile. Hemo took pride in his way of eating and he savored each mouthful before slicing off a new piece.

Amin was never nasty and was further mellowed by his private view of the lively pond, but he thought it his duty to take a shot back at Hemo. "So Hemo, you seeing anyone?"

"Sure, I'm seeing plenty of girls. They just aren't looking back."

Hemo sounded down as soon as the subject of his hunt for feminine companionship was mentioned. Amin felt badly his remark had been a dud, not a jibe. "I'm about to give up on this one I've been with."

"Who is that?" asked Charles.

"Nikki, she works at the bakery in the supermarket."

"And what's wrong with her that you're going to break up?"

Amin hesitated, not sure if he should answer frankly. "I haven't really thought about it, not in a regular, you know, systematic, way. I just realized when you asked me that I should break it off. I don't really like talking with her. She doesn't listen and she doesn't say anything interesting. She just likes to have sex."

"Well, that's not a bad start," Hemo suggested. "I'd take it as a start."

"Yeah, well we started and now I'm seeing we need something else."

"Have you tried doing some other things with her?" Charles asked. "Do you go out? Eat dinner? Meet other couples? Ice skate? There must have been something that got you started. Can you build on it?"

"That's not how Amin works. He can get a new woman any day. He tries 'em out. If they're not perfect, he goes for a new one," Hemo stuck in.

"You know, Hemo, you're right," admitted Amin, "but Charles is right too. I should try harder to make it work. But not with this one. I knew from the start we were not going anywhere for long. She looked so good, I just couldn't say no."

"I couldn't say 'no' either but that doesn't get me anywhere." Hemo admitted more than he intended. His friends knew he did not have an easy time meeting women, but he did not like to show that it bothered him. "I was thinking one of these days something would change. I'm losing my faith, man."

"We ought to put some effort into this. We're all brokenhearted and doing next to nothing about it."

"I'm willing," Hemo responded aloud, while Amin nodded affirmatively and reflectively. "You know what to do?"

"Obviously I don't. I'm in the same sorry state you guys are. Amin had the idea of going on a hike like this with some women. I think that's a really good idea. But it lacks the actual women to go with us."

"What about Sally? Aren't you going to talk to her?" Amin had assumed their conversation about Sally had surprised Charles and that Charles would follow up on the tip that she was interested.

"Sally!" Hemo liked the idea of Charles with Sally. "Is Charles going with Sally? What do you know Amin?"

"I know Sally seemed interested in him and I know they did talk about getting together."

"What Amin knows is that Sally checked me out. She was more interested in husbandly material than in a good time and she did not know me well enough to be sure whether my prospects had improved since high school. It was pretty cool to have her looking into me, but I failed the test."

"Whadda ya mean? You'd make a great husband. What is she looking for?" asked Hemo.

"She never said, but I assumed she would like a lot more than I have to offer. She could be big time. I'm a local guy and like it. I need a woman like that."

"And what was wrong with Natasha?"

"Not a goddam thing. You know, she'd be good on a hike too. She'd keep up with us and have a good time. She sees things I miss, so having her along is like going to a better place. Ah, but she was looking for more than I have to offer too. She wants someone who is devoted to her 24-7. I need a certain part of that for solitude. I have these long discussions with myself. They are not that clever or entertaining, but they help work things out. There are always things to figure out and it is just so strenuous to explain everything to someone else and so boring to hear everything she has to work out in her head. I just want to share the important thoughts ...maybe not even all of those."

"Didn't you love her?" asked Amin. "It always seemed like you did and even now you always sound like she's so special to you."

"Love? It is too easy to say yes or no to that. Too many songs and movies. Maybe too many books about it but I don't know 'cause their not on my reading list. She is the best thing that ever happened to me, yes. Can I live without her? Well, I'll have to and I will. When she decided to leave, some of my enthusiasm went with her. What do you say, Amin. Does love have a consistent meaning in the culture back in Morocco?"

"We have 'love' in our language. It is not exactly the same thing but it is full of misunderstandings. I don't think we worry about it as much. Women may be easier there. I don't know; I left too young to know about them."

"You could ask Sally to hike with us. She's fit and probably has a lot to say," Hemo suggested. "I bet she would be interesting to hear. I promise not to drool when I see her."

"I tell you Sally is not in the picture. But there is someone else I could ask."

"Whoa, 'someone else'!" Hemo punched Charles on the shoulder. "What aren't you telling us? What have you got going?"

"Relax, cowboy. I don't have anything going, not the way you mean. I only mean I could ask her and I think she would appreciate a hike in our forestlands. It's a long story without any chapters you'd find worthwhile. ...You know the cashier at Smiley's?"

"Of course, I know who you mean but I don't know her. You know her?" asked Hemo.

"She seems very nice," added Amin. "Elizabeth, right?"

"Her real name is 'Makeda.' I don't know her but I had a little business deal with her brother. Like I said, I could ask her. I never thought we would date, but this could be a nice thing."

"Knows the brother! Good angle, man! At least I guess it is. I'm not the one to say what works." Hemo's confidence flagged noticeably. "I'd like to know the brother. She seems solid; not just a face."

For a full minute no one spoke, but each was considering Makeda. "She got a wonderful face though," Amin added.

"So I was not thinking of doing anything with her until now. You guys need to revise your approach and come up with a girl to invite on our next one. We'll go again this fall, before it gets too cold. Maybe if you're not thinking about sex so much, you'll find someone different, someone fun. Or someone who may be fun. ...Hold on, was that Route 2 there?"

It was Route 2 and Charles backed-up the van
to follow it. "Just a couple miles to Lowes Store.
That's the trailhead!"

Chapter 14 - Mt. Adams

They parked the van in the lot beside Lowes Store. Charles put the money for parking into a wooden box on a pole. They laced up their hiking shoes. Charles did a hasty inspection. Although he was subtle about it, both his friends were aware he had checked out their equipment. Mainly he wanted to be sure they had sufficient warmth in case it was cold at the higher elevations, and that they had rain protection. The thought of rain made him look skyward to confirm what the radio had said about a clear day. "Mares' tails," he commented, pointing to the high clouds.

Hemo and Amin looked up. Amin asked needlessly "Is that what they call them?"

"My mother liked to talk about clouds. Her father was a sailor and she valued being able to predict the weather from the signs in the sky. 'Mares' tails and mackerel scales make lofty ships carry low sails.' I'm not sure exactly what it means. She didn't explain. I thought it meant seeing those kinds of clouds implied wind was likely. We'll see if it gets windy today."

"I hope it's not too windy. It's already friggin' cold," Hemo complained.

"It's October, man! You don't get this unique kind of spectacular New England color in the summertime. And we just drove north for ninety minutes, and we're climbing a friggin' mountain.

Embrace it! You won't be sweating like last summer, but you'll be warmer once we get moving."

"All right, let's roll!" Hemo answered, anxious to show his enthusiasm. "You need help tying those shoe laces, Amin? You're probably used to some woman tying them for you in the morning."

"I've been ready for ten minutes while you two analyze the weather. I'm a warm climate soul, young and healthy. Let's get exercising."

"My mother would say you're full of beans," said Charles as he led up the trail.

The trail dipped from the parking lot to a swampy area with boulders scattered among the open forest of small black ash trees. Their leaves had already fallen, softening the uneven terrain and hiding small areas of shallow, open water. It was dark because the sun had not climbed above the cliffs nearby the east of the trail. Small streams flowed over the cliff face, not dropping into space like a true waterfall, but running over the surface, feeding a lush growth of moss over many square yards of rocky surface. The hikers had just begun and already felt they were someplace unlike anyplace they had been before.

A little farther on, a rocky overhang in the cliffs protected a dark hole at the bottom which each of the three silently imagined as the den of a different animal: bear, coyote, raccoon. They might have gone closer to see it were really were deep enough for hibernating and might have looked for tracks to see what animal had been there, but the hike was just beginning and they all felt the urge to get somewhere farther and more remote. Finding an animal den so near the parking lot would have been unearned.

The trail turned partly toward the east and worked its way through the swamp on a bed of loose rocks. They went slowly and used their hiking sticks for security but soon climbed gently above the swamp, past the cliffs, through a gate of barbed wire, onto a long grassy rise. The field had been mowed recently and large, round bales were scattered across it. The hikers were moving fast now, feeling the inevitable energy of young men on a cool, clear morning headed into the wilderness, as much as New England could offer that experience.

The trail ran along the edge of the field, several inches to a foot lower than the level of the sod, eroded by boots and rain into a rocky scar. Since there were no trees close by, no leaves softened the footing and the loose rocks were exposed. Their potential to slide or to turn an ankle occupied much of the hikers' attention. It was much harder to walk on the trail than on the field, but all three kept to the track as if there were some moral merit in it.

At the top of the clearing, Charles stopped to look back at the view. The trees on the edge of the field had enough light to leaf all the way to the ground. Those leaves mostly showed a dull russet coloration but a few white oaks dressed in a brighter shade of purple. In one corner, a growth of sumac showed how brightly the red of autumn can burn.

The three hikers had already climbed well above the treetops at the bottom of the opening so they had a view into the distance. They were not facing any major mountains, but they could see a rolling horizon and, in one direction, a cloud fogging a valley as if it had overslept and still wore a coverlet. No one had words for the scene so no one said anything. They stood in a row, each leaning on his hiking stick, each relieved that the hike was underway and was putting on the show they had hoped to find.

Charles unbuttoned his jacket. He would have taken it off but was too lazy to go to that much effort. Hemo had started out underdressed so he was just becoming comfortable. Amin did not make any adjustment. He was getting warm, but he was convinced he was dressed appropriately and did not want to disturb the balance. Charles nodded for him to take the lead. He liked the idea and vowed just to himself to set a strong pace. He opened another barbed wire gate and entered the forest with his friends close behind.

Amin looked back to be sure someone closed the gate. He was struck by the sight of the sun shining through the tall, limp stems left over from the summer forage in the open field, waving with the breeze that ran up the mountainside. He could see the shape of the wind in the shifting shafts of grass, moving in unison where the breeze was pressing. He saw it as the fulfillment of the promise of horsetail clouds. With all the brilliant colors above them, and in the vistas beyond, crying for attention, the gentle browns of the rocks underfoot and their tender, mobile textures most made him feel the passage of a season and the appeal of the exact day he was in.

Hemo reattached the barbed wire fence before he saw Amin looking in his direction. "What?" and he looked back to see if he had just closed the gate on someone coming up the trail.

"Leaves of Grass," said Amin.

"No shit," said Hemo. "What about 'em?"

"It's a poem," Charles answered. "By Walt Whitman. About nature. That's what you meant, didn't you, Amin?"

"Not exactly," said Amin. "It's his whole collection of poems. The title refers to all the poems, the *leaves* of paper they're on, and the insignificance of any one of them. But together they are something to celebrate."

There was no answer to Amin's story. Charles and Hemo leaned on their hiking sticks again and looked at the rustling grasses, appreciating them more since they had been pointed out, until they heard Amin's footsteps leading on.

Two hours and more later, Charles called ahead to Hemo who was in front by then. "My watch says it's lunchtime. This looks like a good place to stop."

"Watch? You brought a watch? I thought you stayed away from such high tech instrumentation on your wilderness jaunts. And why would you want to follow a precise schedule?"

"Good questions, my friend, and ones I can answer if you are patient." He slung off his pack and sat beside it. "I did apply the logic you describe when I was very young. But I once took a camping trip with a few guys, we were probably 14 or 15 at the time, and none of us had a driver's license and my mother agreed to pick us at one o'clock on the third day. It was overcast and we were four hours late but had no idea we were late at all. She had contacted the park ranger but they had not panicked. He was standing next to her car when we came strolling down the hillside, thinking she must have gotten there early. She was good about it and maybe that made me feel worse. But I have always carried the small burden of a watch ever since then. I hope I do not let it command me but I like to consult with it. For example, I do not get hungry so I do not feel any demand for meals. I get thirsty and want something to drink, but I am fed too well to get real hunger. Yet I get bored and look for the distraction of a meal sometimes. My 'hunger' was inspired this time by the nice layout of this little streamside plateau, so I looked at my watch and decided that if we are to eat, we should do it now. And I have a good lunch for us too."

"Yeah, I know. Fresh bread and soft cheese. Do you have cold beer this time? That's all I ask every trip and you never come through."

"And I always say you are welcome to BYOB. I love water in the woods. Funny, I never drink it at home. No, I've brought beans and franks. Let's get a fire going. A fire in the fall smells like the season. When we take the women out, we'll need to cook something for 'em and that starts with a fire. We'll get a more elaborate menu than this, but it's good enough for us."

"Ooh, sounds good to me," Hemo answered.

"I guess it's OK. What kind of beans did you bring? Don't they take a long time to cook?" asked Amin.

"There's only one kind of beans to go with franks and they just need to get heated up. You think Charles doesn't know his business?"

"I didn't mean there was anything wrong with it. Cooking beans out here just seemed funny."

Charles decided to give a straight response. He wondered if he had become tiresome, being a wise guy too much. "You're right, Amin. That would be slow and it would be awkward but this will be really easy. The only equipment we'll need is a spoon for each of us. We cook the franks on a stick and the beans stay in the can. You know how to build a cooking fire?"

"I guess I can start a fire."

"We can do it together. There's not much to it, especially on a dry day like this, but I like to pretend to be a woodsman and have my own tricks for efficiency. Hemo, why don't you pull out that knife and cut us some weenie sticks. You know, with a fork to hold 'em good, green wood, bark peeled off?"

"OK Boss. I can do that. Maybe I can cut our initials into them too."

"And the date would be nice. Today's the eighth, I think. Spell out the month, of course."

While Amin gathered some wood, Charles cleared a space for a fire and placed some stones on two sides, leaving a channel for air flow. Then he cut the lids, except for a hinge about an inch long, on three cans of beans. It was more beans than any of them would want, but it was easiest to have separate cans. He spread his poncho as a dinner table and put out his canteen, three "tin" cups actually made of aluminum, three spoons, some mustard packets, a small jar of relish, a bag of buns, and a package of hot dogs. He collected tinder from the ground, within reach of where he sat.

"Look here, Amin. Here's my system. Maybe you have a better way, but this will work. It is a failure if it requires a second match." He had three piles of tinder separated by size. He crumpled the first pile into a tight wad to maximize the surface area first exposed to the flame. With no further preparation, he lit the wad and a flame six inches high rose up. He quickly placed twigs from the second pile into the flames, wherever they were brightest. The moment that pile was exhausted, he started putting in the larger sticks from the third pile. The flames grew larger still. He began breaking up the material Amin had gathered and carefully placed each stick where it would add the most. Within two minutes after he had struck the match, he sat back and watched the fire continue on its own. "It's more about the labor than the materials."

Hemo came back to the site carrying three sticks. I found a tree full of these three-prong options," he announced.

"Probably a maple," suggested Charles. "They have opposite branches. Turning red was it? Brighter red than the oaks around the field back there?"

"Don't know... yeah, maybe. Something was pretty red. There were a lot of them together right over there," and he pointed to a flat area nearby, glowing in red. "It sure looks bright now. Don't know why I didn't notice it." But he had not simply been unobservant. He had wandered into the maple thicket indirectly and did not have the view they all had now of sunlight passing through the leaves.

"We can roast the hot dogs while the fire is burning down to coals. Then we'll heat up the beans. I hope you don't mind eating in courses." Charles dragged a log near the fire as a bench. It was uneven so he propped one end on another log. "You g' one of those with my name on it yet, Hemo?"

The first round of hot dogs was roasted slowly and carefully, as if an even roast were essential to the quality of the repast. They each smothered that first one in relish and mustard. The fire was building some coals by the time they finished them so Charles handed out the cans of beans, saying he would not be responsible for how they turned out, except for his own. He peeled a long stick and used it to stir his beans so they would be heated moderately evenly. Amin saw this and copied it. Hemo saw Charles' method and ignored it.

The first hot dogs had built the level of hunger rather than reduced it. The second round of hot dogs was cooked with less effort toward quality and the cooks decided to use only one condiment at a time. Charles leaned back and sipped his water after the second 'dog while his beans continued to heat. He waited until they steamed before tasting them. No one managed to consume an entire can, but they all went back for a third 'dog. Charles skipped the bun on his third one but he used the mustard liberally. They had spoken little during the meal although they had felt close to one another for simultaneously sharing both the preparations and the consumption; they were both independent and social which felt good to them.

"Are you sleepy now with that big meal inside you?" asked Hemo as he started kicking at the fire to spread the coals out.

Amin jumped to his feet, strapped on his canteen and picked up his hiking stick. "I'm just getting started."

Charles rose more slowly and stretched his arms up and arched his back in a cartoon yawn. "Ahh, I am so sleepy, but there is so much more to see, I'll get back on the trail with you."

"How do you know what's on this trail?" asked Amin. "I thought you were never here before."

Charles stuffed the remains of the food back into his pack and then tromped on the ashes along with Hemo. "I've never been here before and I do not know specifically what lies ahead, but I am certain whatever is out there will be wondrous. I won't waste a day and a place as fine as this with lying around for peaceful digesting." He knelt beside the former fire site and pressed his hands onto the ashes to be sure they were cold. Then he kicked dirt and leaves around so the site would be entirely invisible. Hemo and Amin watched, understanding his actions, but Charles offered something of an explanation anyway, "I want to deny future anthropologists any knowledge of this expedition." Amin stirred the leaves with his pole. "Hemo, I believe you are in the lead now?" said Charles with a lift at the end of the sentence to make it into a polite question.

The three clattered onward up the stony trail. They expected the colors around them to be their greatest pleasure, but more than that, they were each most pleased by the ability of their bodies to carry them so comfortably beyond everyday experience, beyond the company of other people, beyond the tribulations of their work lives and love lives and financial woes for a day.

Hemo set a rapid pace. He was not trying to demonstrate his vigor; he was just excited by the circumstances. He liked being in the lead, even if he was not actually making any choices about the route. After thirty minutes, he stopped at the edge of a saddle in the trail, to let the others catch up. There had been a sharp rise to reach the saddle so it was a good place for a rest. As Amin and Charles reached him, they all heard the honking of Canada geese overhead. They looked up but there were too many leaves to see the birds though they could easily visualize the V as it passed. As they stood there "watching" the geese, a breeze ran over the saddle and showered them with small yellow leaves. The ground was already covered in them and the sunlight filtered through the ones that were still waiting to dry enough to break free. Amin held out his hands to catch a part of the downpour. They all smiled at his gesture. A leaf settled on Hemo's cap and several on Charles shoulders. Their standing rest lasted no more than two minutes. Charles thought it good policy to make it longer, but he wanted to see what was ahead and stepped away saying, "My turn now."

From the saddle the trail worked its way along a rising ridgeline. The trees were smaller and browner leaved as they gained altitude, but the hikers could see brilliant splashes on the hillsides around them. It was nearing the time they would need to start returning when they broke out of the trees altogether onto a windswept, bushy cap. Hemo and Amin both asked if this was the top of Adams, and Charles answered that it could not be the top; the climb had been much too easy. He knew Mt. Adams had several false peaks, named after various famous Adamses. He had a map in his pack and was about to take it out when he saw what he had hoped all day to find and called out happily "Blueberries! Time for dessert!" Here in the north at this elevation, the berries were as full as early August back in their part of the state.

All three quickly forgot the aches they had been feeling in their legs and set about collecting berries. Charles laid his handkerchief in his cap and tossed most of his collection in there while the others put theirs straight to the gullet. The energy required to collect the berries may have exceeded the energy gained from consuming them, but the dessert, like all desserts, was not intended for efficiency. As they plucked at the bushes, they developed their own techniques for getting the berries into their hands. Hemo tried shaking the ripened branches but did not get much that way, so he switched over to drawing the branch through a circle of his fingers. This produced a fist of dried leaves and small twigs in addition to the berries, and he separated them by blowing on the lot. This method made him suddenly remember the stories he had heard of bears working their way through blueberry patches on New Hampshire mountainsides. He called out, "Amin, Amin!" until Amin answered, and then he called "Charles, Charles," until he answered too. "Look out for bears. No, really, there could be one here. A couple years ago I saw one in the bushes and I heard him first. He was grunting, like." And Charles agreed it was good advice.

"How can a bear get fat eating these tiny berries?" asked Charles to anyone who might be listening. No one answered but Hemo wondered to himself if a bear's eating all the twigs added significantly to the nutritional content.

After 20 minutes or so, Charles settled down on a rocky outcrop to rest his back and look at the view, slowly eating his capful of berries. He contemplated their taste, tart, even though he and his companions had been saying all along how sweet they were. Perhaps it was the tiny seeds that contributed both texture and a complex taste; maybe it was the skins. Too soon his handkerchief was empty and he refolded it and put it back in his pocket. He leaned on one elbow to look down at the display of colors below them and off to the distance. "Are we already getting so used to these bizarre hues of chlorophyll that we don't feel the need to gawk and exclaim about them?" he asked. No one answered but his friends both looked out at the mountainsides guiltily. Stuffing their mouths for twenty minutes with hardly a word brought a faint culpability from the remnants of the sin of gluttony they had never in their lives tried to avoid.

Amin pointed to a long valley marked in bright red that contrasted with the slopes beside it and said simply "Look at that one." Charles marked his direction and saw what he meant so he answered,

"Yeah... nice." Charles had no idea that Amin had a further thought in is head that the rich red looked like blood flowing from a gash in the side of the mountain, and he was wondering what titan, like Atlas, might have inflicted such a wound in the New World.

"Judging by the sun, not my watch, we ought to be heading back. But let's walk close for a few minutes. I have an idea to bring up with you both." Charles' words intrigued his companions although less so for Hemo who knew Charles had a sense of humor that sometimes built on false leads. This time, however, Charles was entirely sincere. He consciously spoke with a fuller voice than normal, pushing from his diaphragm so his words would be heard well despite the need for all three men to watch their footing on the trail. He explained that the experience of having Hemo help on the job had got him thinking about whether he could expand his business model to include a full-time partner. He usually had more requests for jobs than he had time for the work, but it was still risky to take on the responsibility of two livelihoods. So he got to wondering how to do more marketing, get better jobs, longer ones, and ones that paid better. He did not think he could handle that in addition to the regular work and then he realized bringing in Amin to run an office could solve a lot of the problems. He emphasized it was risky to expand so much. He pointed out that he did not know how to make it pay enough to support three people, but that he had thought about it long and hard. He had no papers to show them, but he had his own confidence. They should not think of it as a way to make more money, but as a way to have more say in their work. They would stay friends, and if that was ever in question, they would break up the company. He gave no hint of why he was not too worried about collapsing financially but he had in mind that his cash hoard would make the first year safe, at least, if they just tried to make a reasonable living. "Details come later," he concluded. "There are options to arrange things however we want, within what's possible. For now, just think about it. Think about whether it's worth taking a risk. We'll talk about it again in a few days."

"I don't need any details," Hemo said immediately. "I'm in. I've been lookin' for a risk to take. This is the one."

Amin said simply, "I'm in too. Let's start."

"Don't quit your regular job tonight," Charles warned. "Let's write up a plan. See if it looks good. I think it will. Maybe you can give notice in a week. But remember, we want our business to work in this town, so don't piss off your bosses. Maybe they'll need some work this winter."

"Uh huh. Take this job and shove it!" sang Hemo.

"That's just between us, right Hemo?" asked Amin.

"It was a movie, you know," Charles mentioned. "Did you know that, Amin? It was probably before your time although Whitman was before your time too."

"No man," inserted Hemo. "First it was a song. Johnny Paycheck. Before the movie. Oh do I know that one," and he sang it with a tune and a beat:

> "Take this job and shove it.
> I ain't workin' here no more.
> My woman done left and took
> all the reason I was working for ya,
> better not try and stand in my way,
> 'cause I'm walkin' out the door...

Whoops, I shouldda sung a different verse. Charles might be a little sensitive about the woman walkin' out the door."

"Fact is, Hemo, she did walk out the door. If I had a better job, she mightta wanted to stay more, but I think it was other things. Anyway, I'm over it."

"No you ain't. Yer needs a woman."

"Umm, don't I know it."

"Yer needs that woman. Natasha."

"I hope she's not the one I need 'cause I'm not goin' to get her."

"Well Sally ain't a bad second choice."

"I'm not gettin' her either. But next trip out here, we'll all have a woman to know, right? If you don't want to think about our business, think about who you're gonna bring." That suggestion turned all their thoughts inward for the next couple miles of trail.

The mountain on the opposite side of the road, that is, of where they presumed the road to be, got closer as they reached the lower slopes. They could guess how far they needed to go to reach where the two mountains came together and as that point approached, they took a more direct route, crashing down the steep slope, using their muscles only to keep from falling. Hemo reached the bottom first. He let his momentum carry him to the middle of the road, a smooth two lanes with ample shoulders. He supposed it was the right road, the one where they had parked. There weren't many roads this substantial in the area. Charles and Amin followed soon, but Hemo was already resting on the road bank. His breath had not yet calmed to normal. Charles and Amin both fell near Hemo. All of them could feel their legs twitching from the long day of hiking and the final exertions. Amin took a drink from his canteen and passed it around. They were not hot, but the water was refreshing.

Without a thought as to which direction to take, Charles led to the left, also assuming they were on the right road, but having little opinion on how far they might be from the van. The tight valley where they were walking was deep in shade although the sky above remained bright enough to show the sun had not really set. It took fifteen minutes, about a mile, to reach a pass where they could see into the distance. None of them recognized any particular part of the scene. Charles asked if he should take out the map and see if he could locate their spot, but no one cared that much. They knew they would continue in this direction a while no matter what the map appeared to show. The sun was getting close to the natural horizon as they left the pass. A few clouds were turning ruby as if reflecting the colors on the mountainside.

"'Red sky at night; sailors' delight. Red sky in morning, sailors take warning.' Further wisdom from my mother," quoted Charles.

"But that's not what you said this morning. You said to expect winds or storms and now you say to 'take delight'," Hemo remarked without conviction.

"Maybe these things only work in the ocean," Amin suggested.

A car passed. Hemo wondered if they should try to hitch a ride, but he made no motion to the driver. He thought he might raise the idea before the next car came.

"Over there!" Charles pointed toward something shiny in the distance. "Around this hill... See where the road is? That's Lowe's store. This is Adams here on our left. Ten minutes-- we'll be back."

"Is the store open? We could get a drink there."

"I don't know. I doubt they stay open this late."

"I could use some coffee."

The three were getting cool with the evening shade, the easy walk on the roadway, and their sweaty clothes. They were not uncomfortable exactly; just ready to finish the day and climb into a van with padded seats and a heater. Hemo picked up his pace as they came in view of the van. He stood by the door waiting for Charles to bring the key. Charles opened the passenger side first, not to torture Hemo any further, and they all settled deeply into their seats. Charles took a deep breath before turning the key in the ignition. The muscle fibers in his thighs were still twitching although he had not noticed it on the road. Hemo checked his phone for messages.

"Goddam!" Hemo swore, holding the phone to his ear. "This is some kind of call for you Charles. You telling people I'm your secretary?"

"Who is it?" Charles asked. As Hemo knew, he had often given Hemo's number out but no one had ever used it before.

"Some guy sounds named 'Bekele,' it sounds like. Says you need to get over to his house."

"When did he send it?"

"Umm, 4:32. Not too long ago. Wait, there's another one from the same guy. This one's at 4:44."

"You know Elizabeth? The cashier at the diner? That's her brother. I helped with his landlord. Got him a court order when he was being evicted. Can you call him back? See if he wants me to come by tonight. Maybe he lost his copy of the court papers or something."

"Hold on. I'll call. Shouldn't Amin do this if he gonna be the clerk in our outfit?"

"He's not on the payroll yet. It's your phone."

"No answer anyway... Hello, hello. This is Hemo. I'm Charles' friend. You left a message on my phone for him. Call me back. We're by the phone now."

"Well done. Amin, he may be competing for your job."

Chapter 15 - Eviction

Bekele did not call back during the ninety minutes it took the three hikers to get back to town, and both Amin and Hemo were curious enough about the call that they agreed to go along to Bekele's house instead of being dropped off. They both harbored an interest in meeting outside the diner with the woman they knew as Elizabeth.

While still a block away from Bekele's apartment, the three in the van could see something was happening on the unmown lawn in front of his building. The headlights from a green pickup were shining into the yard where random furniture and several neat stacks of clothes were lying about. Charles parked well before he reached the scene and sat quietly for a half minute to be sure he was not too emotional going into the situation. Neither Hemo nor Amin said anything. They both jumped out of the van as soon as Charles unlatched his door. Before they reached the lit space, they all noticed that a car from the sheriff's office was parked nearby. Charles was relieved to see it. Once inside the scene lit by the pickup, they could not see anything beyond the stark light. It appeared at first that the drama had already occurred and they were seeing its silent remains, but on one side there was a little movement and even a little sound. Charles went over to huddled shapes of Makeda, her mother, Bekele's wife, and his two small children. Makeda and

Bekele's wife were trying to console the mother, who was sobbing discretely. As soon as she saw Charles approaching, she stopped her sounds and hid her face behind a white, lacey fabric hanging around her neck. Makeda looked up at Charles with an angry expression made harsher by the lighting. "You did not help us," she accused in calm tones.

"Isn't the sheriff here?" Charles asked. She waved toward the apartment but was already redirecting her attention back to her mother softly.

Charles walked quickly to the apartment door and knocked. Hemo and Amin stood close behind him, still silent. No one came to the door so Charles opened it and went inside. He could hear men's voices but not their words. It sounded like someone giving orders. He hoped it was the sheriff telling off the landlord. He went upstairs, toward the voices, and soon saw a sheriff's deputy. He was indeed giving orders, but they were directed at Bekele, telling him to get everything outside tonight, adding that he was tired of waiting and watching, and wanted to get home. Charles was disappointed in the words and thought their amateurism was consistent with the deputy's appearance: overweight, his shirttail hanging loosely, and a baseball-style cap with a folded brim stained with sweat. He knocked on the doorframe. The deputy turned at the sound. Charles stepped into the room and saw three other men. He recognized one of them as the big-bellied thug who had searched his house.

He had not shaved for a few days and looked different in the face, but the tattoo on his neck made Charles sure it was the same man. One of the others was really tall and thin in a wiry way. His tats covered one arm. The third man was the oldest, some grey showed in his long hair, and his face was heavily tanned and wrinkled. A cigarette hung from his lips and a ring from his earlobe.

"Hello," Charles waved at Bekele and looked back to the Deputy. "My name is Charles and I am a friend of Bekele. I have a copy of a court order that prohibits evicting him before his lease expires next February. May I get it for you?"

"Who the fuck are you?" he answered.

The big bellied man said, "He's the girl's boyfriend."

"No, I am not anybody's boyfriend. I came here at Bekele's request. He has..."

Charles was cut off by the deputy. "Get the fuck out of here. This is none of your business."

"Just let me show you..."

"I'm not going to ask you again. Get out of here and stay out. This man does not live here anymore and you are trespassing."

Charles looked the deputy in the face without flinching. He nodded slightly and turned around to face Hemo and Amin who were standing too close to him. They backed up and all three went down the stairs. Before they were outside, they heard three sets of heavy footfalls following them.

Charles headed back to the van to call the lawyer, but one of the men grabbed his arm and spun him around. Hemo stood close beside Charles; Amin stood behind them.

"Look, I know you," said the man Charles had recognized. "You're Charles with the lousy house we looked through once."

Charles thought of apologizing for not cleaning the house before their visit, but he thought this was a poor time for sarcasm. He thought of being cool, saying something like "How do you do?" but that too sounded unlikely to help. He delayed so long in answering that he decided not to answer at all. But suddenly the right words came to mind.

"Yes, I am Charles. I am sorry, I don't recall your name?"

"I never said... You've been alright with us. Go home. No one is going to get hurt here."

Charles answered "Okay. Thanks for your advice," and remained where he was.

"Like the man said," the big-bellied man continued, "you're trespassing until you get your ass on the street."

The six men formed a tense tableau. "You know whose land you're trespassing on?"

"I can move to the street, but I will need a lot more explanation before this is over."

"Don't ya see, this *is* over. This is Robbie's apartments. We work for Robbie. That deputy in there works for Robbie. These Africans got to go somewhere else. Just like you got to go somewhere else. I mean right now. Go home, Charles. After tonight they won't be comin' back here. You can get yourself another girlfriend."

Charles did not answer because he did not trust anything he would say could help anything. He led his team back to the van where he borrowed Hemo's phone and called the lawyer. The lawyer's message said he would not be available until Monday. Charles left his own message, trying to sound as desperate as possible. He leaned forward and drummed lightly on the dashboard while he wondered whom else he could call. The presence of the deputy seemed to leave out any appeal to the police department. The deputy probably knew better than he how to handle them. As they sat there, a few more boxes were taken out of the house and set on the lawn. The deputy stood by while the big-bellied man talked with Bekele, and then the deputy drove away.

The big-bellied thug started to shove Bekele toward the boxes. The other men began to pile the furniture roughly into one of the pick-up trucks. Makeda's mother screamed briefly, but not very loudly. Hemo was the first one out of the van. Charles ran around the front and grabbed Hemo. "You're right,

Hemo. We gonna have to step in here. Let's think a moment about how to do that."

Hemo stuck out his chin and looked at the confrontation with Bekele. "We ought to get Amin out of here. This is no place for him. He'll be in the way. His heart's okay but he'll just be something more to worry about."

Amin came up to them and put an arm on their shoulders conspiratorially. Charles faced him. "Amin, get those women and his kids out of here. Take them to a motel somewhere. I'll pay for it. Tell them that. We'll stay with Bekele. You stay with them. Keep your phone close."

Bekele tripped over the boxes and lay on the ground. Makeda ran over to him and stood between him and the big-bellied man. Charles handed his keys to Amin and ran off. Amin held Hemo for a moment, staring at Charles' back. He handed Hemo something and then went to the van, started the engine and drove close to the apartment. Hemo walked calmly toward Charles.

Makeda was not yet hysterical, but she was in no mood to discuss a strategy. Bekele was quiet. When Charles got close, the big-bellied man stopped pressing Bekele and addressed Charles. "Yer trespassing again." His two partners stopped their loading and watched.

Charles did not speak to the big-bellied man. "Bekele, are you all right?" It was a formality to ask.

Bekele was getting up and showed no injury. "Makeda, we'll help Bekele take care of your things. You ought to get the rest of your family someplace for the night. My friend in the van will drive you to a motel."

"You want to help. I believe you. But you can't do anything for us," she spit back at him.

"This is not a good place for your mother tonight."

The big-bellied man interrupted, "We got a place for all of them. We're taking them and their junk there tonight. They don't have another night in this town."

Finally Charles spoke to him directly, "You don't need to make this any uglier. Let the old women have her peace..."

"That's not how it goin' down. I told you to get out of here and you're going to do it."

"It's not that easy to bully us in America these days, even if some idiot sheriff's deputy is on the payroll. We have your trucks' license numbers so this will not end tonight for you."

Makeda's mother began to sob loudly. One of the men blocked her path to the van. Makeda saw him and realized the stress itself was a danger for her mother. Amin came across the lawn to the mother and took her arm. He led her to the van, walking slowly around the man who had blocked her way. Bekele's wife followed closely with her children. Makeda let them go but did not follow her.

The big-bellied man told the tall man to "get Robbie on the horn." When he stepped away from the group to talk to Robbie, Charles spoke to Makeda and Bekele.

"I am really sorry about this. We can work on some solution, but standing here at night with these gentlemen is no way to conduct business. Please let my friend take you, Makeda, someplace quiet and safe for the night. Hemo and I will stand by Bekele."

Bekele said he did not see what they could do but he agreed Makeda should go to a motel and she gave in to the idea, mainly because she had no better idea for such an intractable situation.

Amin stood by the van, keeping the two women inside company and watching for any sign from Charles.

Makeda went over to the boxes and drew out some things. Charles wanted her to hurry but did not want to hurry her. She made a small mound of things and Charles waved Amin over to put it in the van. He did not want to break up his small defensive huddle. Amin immediately jogged over to the things Makeda was gathering. When he picked as much as he could balance on his arms, the tall man put a hand on him, not forcefully, just enough to communicate, to say he should not carry them to the van. Hemo was quick to push himself between them. He stared directly into the man's face from twelve inches away. Amin walked to the van while Hemo shifted his position to remain between him and the man. Makeda stopped sorting through the piles and looked to the van. She started toward it and the older man moved toward her. Charles spoke up, "You know, if you touch her, no matter how lightly, it'll be on. There are witnesses in all these windows out here and I am fully ready to bleed for their entertainment. It is not worth it. She is just going to get out of the way. *Not one finger on her.*" Suddenly Makeda bolted toward the van. Bekele watched silently. Charles waved over his shoulder for Amin to leave and the van spun its tires a moment later on the way out.

Big Belly came running and shouting back to the group. He held the phone in front of himself, as if he did not want the call to fall out. He was screaming that no one should leave but everyone else could see that it was too late to stop them. The tall man did not say anything but the older one said it was just a couple of women and they still had Bekele. Big Belly told him to shut up and he explained to the phone that the women had left in a van. He apparently got his instructions and passed them on: "No one else leaves! So, Charles, I thought you knew how to be a good fellow, but I see you are part of the problem. Call your buddy up and tell him to get his ass back here and to bring those women with him. You'll be glad he did."

"Can't do it," Charles answered. "He doesn't have a phone with him and I don't even know where he's going. I told him not to tell me. But don't worry, we're not going anywhere as long as Bekele's possessions are lying on the grass out here."

Big Belly walked back into the shadows and muttered into his phone. He had a tendency to mutter his curses more loudly or more clearly or both because the only words that reached the others were vulgar. Charles used the time to reassure Bekele. "Don't worry about Makeda and your wife. My friend is a good man. They will be safe and comfortable. We just need to get your things back in the apartment. Then I'll reach my lawyer on Monday. We can get out of this just fine; back to the way it was a couple days ago." Bekele mostly nodded. He did not say any clear sentences and he hardly looked up. Even so, Charles thought he saw some improvement in his demeanor. He had lost confidence in Charles, but had some hope of a resolution without utter disaster for his family.

When Big Belly returned, he spoke mostly to his partners. "No one leaves until Robbie gets here. No one! Understand? Be hear in twenty, he says." Then he directed himself mostly to Charles. "Everyone inside." And back to the older man: "Turn off the fuckin' lights!"

Charles spoke quietly to Bekele while Hemo kept an eye on the others. "I think we should stay out here. Your stuff will be safer if we're watching over it. Besides, there are witnesses to whatever happens here." Bekele nodded with such a small movement, Charles was not sure whether he was agreeing or disagreeing.

Suddenly the truck lights went off and they all were blind. There were no street lights nearby, but eventually their eyes adjusted and they could see well enough to function. "Inside," Big Belly commanded.

"We staying here," said Charles.

"You need some encouragement? I can arrange that."

"Do you want the ruckus before Robbie gets here?" Charles asked. "There will be more than one slob of a deputy coming if we do it out here."

"Son of a bitch! You just want a whuppin' and yer goin' to get it sooner or later."

"Let's make it later."

"Not smart; not smart at all."

"I have to agree with you on that," answered Charles. He pulled a couple chairs out of the furniture pile and offered one to Bekele. "Did you show the deputy your court order?"

"He took it. He didn't care what it said."

"I think he cared. That's why he took it. I have another copy and the lawyer has one. So he didn't claim to have some new papers?"

"He says he had something telling him to take the apartment from us. He said we had been warned."

"Did anyone hurt you or the rest of your family?"

"No. They did not hit anyone. Makeda tried to stop them from packing her things so they pushed her away, but they didn't hurt her."

Hemo saw it as his job to watch the thugs for any threatening moves, even though it now seemed they were all just waiting. He took a position where he could see everyone and he planned how to meet them if it came to that. He thought he could handle the big-bellied one and the old one on his own. If he needed to take two of them, he would hit the legs on one first and that would gain time to hit the other while the first one was figuring what to do. They were guys with big mouths, not fighters. Charles could deal with the tall one. Charles was handy enough. Bekele needed to stay out of the way. Defending him would make it harder. He looked for weapons. He knew it was best to avoid escalating the confrontation but prudent to be ready for it. No sign of a pistol. If they drew a knife, Hemo would be all in. He needed to tell Charles his plan. He moved slowly to Charles, watching the others as casually as possible. His hand swept across his thigh and he noticed a lump; it was whatever Amin had given him. His curiosity exceeded his desire to share his plan and he took out Amin's object. He held it to the light as well as possible and turned it over. As far as he could tell, it was nothing; a hard ball of nothing at all. He was about to toss it aside but thought it might be something to Charles. He reached Charles and whispered "Hey, man. Take the tall dude. I got the others, no sweat. Look out for a blade, you know."

Charles looked at the three men. They were engaged in their own confabulation. He assessed their likely strengths. "Got it, Hemo," he whispered back. And he, too, looked into the pile of Bekele's possessions for something that might serve for a club.

A car sped down the street and pulled up to the apartments. It sat idling its engine and then reparked so its lights flooded the yard. It had been less than fifteen minutes since the call with Robbie. Two car doors opened and closed. Two figures walked into the light and came across the yard. Big Belly went out to meet them. They all came back to Charles.

Big Belly made the introductions. "Charles, this is a couple friends of Robbie and me. They just here to watch."

"Sure," said Charles firmly. "Me too."

They all stood facing each other, but separated by the piles of clothing and bedding. Nervous energy pulsed through Hemo. "Charles!" he called at the level of a stage whisper. "That fuckin' Amin's crazy. Before he left, he gave me a big brown nut. Not the kind you eat; just some piece of crap he found on the ground. Something's the matter with him."

"Round? Three-fourths of an inch across? Brown, kinda rough surface."

"That's it."

"He gave that to you just before he left or some time before?"

"Just as he was leavin'. Should I give it to you?"

"Yeah, gimme it. Don't worry about Amin. He's a good man."

Another car came up the street. The sound of women's voice called out Charles' name. Charles liked where he was standing so he just called back. "Yeah, I'm here."

Six women came into the yard, still calling Charles' name. They followed his voice. One of them said, "Amin sent us. He said we should mob the crow."

"Right now we're waiting for Robbie. He's the crow. Any of you know him?"

A couple voices said they knew who he was but no one said they knew him. Charles liked the idea of these women being here. It might reduce tensions.

Big Belly's now recognizable voice laughed as they came into view. "Girls? You sent for girls? What a boner! I dunno; maybe you get out of it tonight, but Robbie don't lose, not in front of anybody. You gonna pay worse if he do this twice. You! You personally, Mr. Charles man."

A pick-up truck arrived. In the back were four more men. Three came out of the cab. One of them shouted out "Hinkley!"

The big-bellied man answered "Over here, Robbie."

Robbie walked slowly across the yard. "Who's the tenant?" Charles could not see the features of Robbie's face or of any of the other newcomers standing in front of the car headlights, but he could see the silhouette of Hinkley point to Bekele.

Charles felt a soft hand weave into the hair on the back of his head. He did not need to turn around to know whose hand it was: Natasha's. "Don't worry," she whispered into his ear. "There's plenty more on the way." Charles was charged by her touch and her voice coming from her invisible throat. He stuck his hand into his pocket and fingered the gall Hemo had given him.

Robbie went up to Bekele. He put something in his mouth and chewed for a few seconds. Bekele took a step backward and stumbled on something, but he did not fall down. Charles still could not see Robbie's face clearly, but he could see Robbie was a little shorter than average and fat, but he strode confidently and spoke with authority. "You leaving here tonight, right? I got you a place to stay. These women din't offer your family nothin'. They just here for the show. Don't need no show. Just get in the truck and we'll put you up for the night. Call your wife and tell her we're coming to get her a room."

Bekele answered just as Charles would have scripted him. "I have a court order. It says I can stay here. I have a lease."

"That right, Hinkley? He have a court order?"

"He had some bogus bit of paper the sheriff office said was nothing. No, he don't have no court order."

"Hinkley! Whaddar all these folks here for?"

"That one's the one that brought 'em. He sent the rest of the family away too." Hinkley held his point at Charles.

Robbie studied Charles; the light favored his angle of view more than Charles'. "You in charge of these trespassers?"

Two more cars arrived. Charles could not easily count how many people got out of them; they were full. This time it was young men, a few carrying things that could have been baseball bats or tire irons. Someone called out "Amin sent us. We're here to see Charles."

Charles answered with a quick "Yo!" He asked Hemo to go over to them and keep them calm. He spoke to Hemo too quietly for Robbie to hear. Then he turned to Robbie who had not looked toward the new arrivals but had waited patiently for Charles to answer. "No, I'm not in charge of anybody. I don't even know who most of these people are. I didn't even ask them to come." Charles remembered that Natasha was there. He knew her well enough but could not imagine how she got mixed up in the affair. There was too much going on and he did not want to think about her just then. "But Bekele is my friend and I am here to be sure his rights are honored."

"Rights? You a lawyer? I heard his lawyer was out of town this weekend. Not even on his cellphone. I wouldda called him but, well, I couldn't."

"No, I'm no lawyer but I know there is some minimum of..."

"Wait a minute. I know you! You're a painter, ain't cha? Hinkley, I know him! This here's the guy that named my granddaughter! You know, little Seneca? Right, Charles? That your idea?"

"Seneca... Oh yeah! Last spring. Tamara's your daughter? Nice girl."

"My stepdaughter. We met when you came by to paint the house. Tamara liked you, I guess, so she named her baby for you. Hinkley, this guy's alright, isn't he? What do we need any trouble?"

"Whatever you say. It's your place," Hinkley answered.

Robbie came over to Charles and put his arm around him, hugging him close. Charles could feel the strength in his beefy arm.

"Look at all this. Just to clean out one apartment." He stopped to watch another vehicle arrive. It was Charles' van. Again several people came running out. Amin spoke to Hemo a moment and then walked briskly up to Charles. He handed him a piece of folder of papers. As Charles took the folder, he saw how Amin's hand was shaking.

"I know a girl named Sandy who works at the courthouse. Here's a copy of the court order and the lease agreement. She's sitting by her phone. She'll have the Staties here if I don't call her back within five minutes." Amin did not look toward Robbie but he spoke so Robbie could hear.

"Thank you," Charles answered. He avoided saying Amin's name. "Five minutes? Hold on a moment. I believe the landowner here misunderstood the court order." He handed the file to Robbie. "May we move Bekele's things back inside?"

Robbie dropped his arm from Charles. He regarded the folder in Charles hand. "Hinkley, did you check those papers yourself? Maybe they weren't the right ones you had. Do these people read English? Just an honest mistake maybe. Charles, you're sure these are in order? What's the rush? The lease won't last forever. When's it run out? Don't matter. Let's get a drink, Charles. Whadda ya say?"

"You seem to be an interesting fellow," Charles answered sincerely. "Give my regards to your family. Tonight, I need to help Bekele get settled back in. Hinkley there knows my address. I guess your wife does too. Let me know if you'd like a drink on another night," and he held out his hand for a shake.

Robbie stared at the outstretched hand a few seconds. Charles did not waver. Robbie shook it and said, "Please give Sandy a call to say this is resolved."

"Sure," Charles added. "I'll give her a call now. Thank her for monitoring things from her end. And take these papers back to the courthouse.   I think we're through with them for now."   Charles took the gall from his pocket and handed it to Amin. Amin put it in his own pocket quickly, almost surreptitiously, but maybe he was just being private with it.

Natasha again touched Charles from behind, rubbing his back. Charles turned to face her. "Thanks for coming, Natasha," was all he could get out. He could not start a conversation in the midst of the melee. He touched her cheek and smiled in a way intended to communicate he still cared about her, even if it was not clear what might be meant by "love," and he hoped the light from her position was sufficient for her to see it. He pulled away and looked for Bekele. "Bekele! Bekele! C'mer man. We should thank all these people and send them away. How much help do you want getting back in? You can call your wife now, right? Should I send Amin to pick her up? Maybe you want to go to her in the motel tonight and face setting up the house tomorrow. I can find someone to stay in your house tonight to watch over it." As Charles' ideas evolved, Bekele stood silently. He was listening and thinking through the ideas, but was not ready to commit to anything too fast.

All he said was "Yes, that would be best for tonight. Stay at the motel."

Charles put two fingers in his mouth and let out his shrill whistle. "Over here, please!" he called out, "Everyone! Bekele has a few words for you."

On Monday Charles went home for a lunch break and made a call to a former client, Mrs. Bowers, and offered to bring her family a cake for dinner that night to celebrate her young granddaughter, Seneca, whom he just heard about. She was very surprised to hear from him and to have him bring a cake, but she did not say "no." She told him to come by at seven-thirty, so after finishing work for the day Charles bought a cake with heavy white frosting and the word "CONGRATULATIONS" written in red at the supermarket and stayed to eat a piece with them. Robbie was there, quiet and cordial. He clearly liked cake and Mrs. Bowers said over and over how much she liked his painting job. She had friends who were jealous of the clean look of her house but she did not want to be superior to them so she was giving them Charles' name to call for their own painting work. Charles said he would give a discount to anyone who was recommended by Mrs. Bowers.

After the cake, Charles went home and up onto the attic to check on his stash of cash. He had made withdrawals from it a few times, including $500 for the lawyer, but it was still bigger than any foreseeable costs. Sitting in the attic, with only a flashlight held between his teeth for illumination, he made a little pile to represent six months' rent on an office for his expanded company, a pile for a computer to go in the office, and small pile for a Skilsaw. A huge amount remained. He made a pile to represent a year of tuition. He was thinking of that for Makeda but he thought he should call Sally to see how to check into financial aid for her. He could not think of any more piles to make. He might need a couple months' salaries to get the business going. He put the money back in its place. And there was still the other stash buried in his house.

All this wealth would bring him freedom. He would be embarrassed when it brought him respect. He could not share his secret or shape his aspirations honestly with anyone. The money isolated him. It was an odd and uncomfortable feeling, but not uncomfortable enough to stop using the lucre.

Back in the living room, he looked up Sally's number on the internet. Before he punched it in, he thought about her, the woman he was calling. He thought of her sitting in his living room as she had done once. Had she become a credible partner now that he had prospects? He would soon have a business. Nothing stood in the way. He was known in their town now as the guy who had stood up to Robbie and gotten away with it. He wanted to look into her perfect face and feel her thighs beneath his fingers and have her want him to be hers. If she decided to come over after his call tonight, she might be wearing tight jeans or, maybe, shorts. Those shapely calves would be enough to incite him from across the room. Sally! Here! His! Why not? Yes, he wanted that but it also disgusted him. If he won her by his momentary achievement, he would need more achievements to keep her. He could not see he had changed into a person of substance, just been terribly lucky. And if she did reduce herself to accepting a small life in a small town, and did not demand more from him than he had to give, more magical accomplishments, would he still think of her as the goddess she seemed in high school? She would be a teenager's wish fulfilled, a fantasy, not a real person to live beside him. He wanted her tonight, but he did not want her for the future.

What he wanted was Natasha. He wanted to wake up beside her and see her soft face in the morning light, relaxed in his company with no intention of going anywhere. One motionless finger firmly on the side of her naked hip would satisfy him.

Why was he thinking of calling Sally rather than to help Makeda in whatever was needed next? He hardly knew her, Makeda, but felt as if he did and as if she was just the sort of dependable woman a man would love for her beauty and would love forever for her clear-eyed kindness. He felt that but he had always realized she was only another form of immature dream for him. She lacked that reality Natasha exuded, that made you aware of Natasha whenever she was in the room and wished for when she was not.

He began to think the money may have served another purpose. It had solved the problem of getting his business going, of having a job each day. He did not need to scramble for work. Amin would do the things he disliked about having a business and that took up more time than they should because he was not dedicated to them and that gave him stress because he was always behind on them. He could be a better partner to Natasha. He could be with her more and do more with her. He could be more responsive.

He looked up Natasha's number in his small notebook. He had not called her since she left. Her number was still stuck in his head, but he was not absolutely sure he had it right. She answered on the second ring.

"Hello Charles."

"Natasha. Nice to hear your voice. Thanks for coming to that fiasco the other night. Strange. wasn't it?"

"It was wonderful. Didn't everything turn out right?"

"Yeah, yeah, every... For Bekele and his family... For now. They still need to find another place to live. That's not easy around here. He doesn't want to leave 'cause he likes his job."

"I heard you were there for Elizabeth, not Bekele."

"Yes, in a way I was, I suppose. I mean, yes, I got involved to help Elizabeth. Makeda is her actual name. But I don't have any real relationship with her. I just got it in my head to help her."

"So it's over with her?"

"No it's not over. Nothing ever started."

"Anyway, it was exciting that night."

"The most exciting thing was your hand on my back." Charles regretted lying about this. He had liked feeling her touch but he had fought off his appreciation to deal with the practical matters at hand.

He knew his comment would sound false, but she had
left such an easy opening.

"Oh yeah. I believe that."

"Natasha..."

"Yes."

"I was calling to ask if you'd like to have dinner,
you know, we could talk."

"Because of the thrill I gave you that night?"

"No, not because of that. I miss you. But not
because of that either. I know you left for good
reasons, even if they were subtle. I think I know what
they were and I think I can do better."

"Oh? What were my good reasons?"

"I wasn't committed enough. I wasn't
uncommitted; it just wasn't in me to be half a couple all
the time. I wasn't a good partner that way."

"Not bad. You were paying attention. But you
didn't do anything wrong. That's who you are. I need
someone just a tiny bit different from you."

"I have probably not changed, but my
circumstances have changed that tiny bit." "Damn," he
thought, "I'm giving her hints about the money."

"You mean you have matured in the last few
months?"

"I guess it would sound pretty bad to say that.
No, I shouldn't claim that, but I suffered without you.
I did not want to look for anyone else, but a couple
ideas came up about other women and there was
nothing interesting those ideas. I don't want to be on

248

my own and I don't want a woman unless that woman is you."

"Sounds like a marriage proposal."

"Damn sure did sound like one but it wasn't. We need to get together. You need to see if I can deliver what I think I want with you, what I think you want."

"But Charles, Honey, I miss you very much too and yet I cannot think you could change that tiny bit I need."

"Good. At least good enough; good enough for now. We'll have dinner... in a nice place. Talk a bit about *us* and about lots of other things. Here's another thing, Hemo and Amin and I are planning a hike up Mt Adams and we'd like you to come along. We already went up there to scout it out."

"Hemo and Amin want me to go along?"

"They like you a lot, everyone does, I'm sure. They would each have a woman too. Right at the moment, you're the only one of the women we have identified."

"Amin doesn't have a girlfriend?"

"Right. Not one for this kind of friendship."

"Charles, Charles... You are still Charles, aren't you? You still love to work on your own. You have your convictions that cannot be challenged. You are a friend to every bird with a broken wing, to puppies without a home, and to beautiful, innocent, foreign-born waitresses. You don't have space in that big heart to settle on one selfish woman."

"We can try it again with the knowledge we gained from before and the knowledge of living alone afterwards. Starts with a dinner together."

"No Charles. Not with me. I know you. I like you a lot. And I know me. If our time together and our time apart have taught me about us, they have taught me we do not belong together. I don't want to be on Facebook together or reading the same books or going to dinner. We are exes on good terms. I've got to move on."

Charles had no more words for her. He thought of saying "...and no hikes in the Presidential Range" but he was afraid she might say she would go.

"'Exes on good terms.' Let's be on good terms. I'll be looking for you at things that aren't dates, Dear."

"Do that, Charles. Good night."

The telephone switched to a dial tone. Charles turned off the phone, but the room did not feel quieter. He stretched forward and switched off the lamp. Then he leaned back in his chair, soft and large. A pattern of parallelograms on the floor informed him there was a bright moon out. Was the moonlight disturbing his silence? If Natasha were right and solitude his friend, why was he so uncomfortable? He turned sideways in the chair with his knees hooked over one arm and his back braced against the other. He felt like a child in the embrace of well-worn but animate furniture. When the word "embrace" reached his consciousness, he rebelled against it by rotating himself further, raising his legs across the back of the chair while his head hung off the seat so what he saw of the room was upside-down. This helped changed his frame of mind-- to the knotty question of handling his pile of cash.

The cash was dangerous-- Robbie was calm now but his menace could certainly revive if the money showed up. Too, the government might get wind of it and ruin him. Would either of these possibilities drag down his friends? For his own soul, he was surprised to feel very little concern... He would keep his friends uninformed. Even paying them in cash would involve them. His soul let him be dishonest even with them if it were in their best interest... In theory he could put a substantial part of the trove into a charitable foundation. He could fake receiving cash donations and get past the IRS although Robbie might see through it... He could at least safely use cash to buy tools. Maybe including a computer for Amin's office. Altogether that might use up, say, $10,000 in the first year and less going forward... It was a terrible waste of interest payments to stash it away as cash and dribble it out over the years but it would be so risky to get greedy about it... Could he make the business profitable with two employees if he did not rely on the treasure? ...And what of a wife? She would have to see what he was doing if he used much of it... The woman question brought back the stress that had him lying inverted in his chair.

He twisted and scooted himself into a normal sitting position. He checked at his watch but could not read it. The moonlight was near and he turned his watch face to capture as much of it as possible but the indirect light was not bright enough to let him read the time. He hesitated to move into the direct light, as if his soft, old chair were a small boat on a cold sea or the sharp light on the floor was hot enough to scorch his bare feet in a flash. He calculated backward from the last time he knew the time and decided it was between nine and ten o'clock-- still too early to go to bed. He would toss sleeplessly for hours, getting just enough rest to fail longer in getting real sleep. It was too late to go to the diner for a slice of pie a la mode, although that came close to being his best idea for action. It would be a good time to sit in the dark and play blues on the saxophone if he had a saxophone and knew how to play it well enough to become lost in the sounds of a pentatonic scale.

He seemed stuck in reality until the idea of leaving sobriety occurred to him. Unfortunately he had no hard liquor in the house and he could not imagine drinking enough beer to escape his mood.

He regarded the moonlight again. It had moved noticeably. He focused on one edge, where it aligned with a certain stripe on the carpet. He could see the light moving; it was slow; he did not sense the movement, but every moment it was farther from the window than the moment before, closer to the wall where he knew it would change its shape into a different set of parallelograms. The same moon, the same window, seen from the same angle of his chair, but different nonetheless; changed in a way that did not matter in itself, but in a way that proved the passage of time far better than the stripe in the rug, closer to the moment when the moon drops below the treetops and no longer sends its beams into Charles' house and he is completely in the shadows of night to accompany the silence and utter solitude.

O see ye not yon narrow road
So beset wi' thorns and briers?
That is the path of Righteousness,
Though after it but few inquires.

And see ye not yon braid, braid road
That lies across the lily leaves?
That is the path of Wickedness,
Though some call it the Road to Heaven.

And see not ye that bonny road,
That winds about the fernie brae?
That is the road to fair Elfland,
Where thou and I this night maun gae.

from *Thomas the Rhymer*
Anonymous, 17th Century, but sometimes
attributed to Sir Walter Scott, 1771- 1832